Finding Justice
by

Kathi Daley

D1176686

Acknowledgments

I want to thank the very talented Jessica Fischer for the cover art.

I so appreciate Bruce Curran, who is always ready and willing to answer my cyber questions, Jayme Maness who takes charge of book clubs and other reader events, and Peggy Hyndman for helping sleuth out those pesky typos.

And, of course, thanks to the readers and bloggers in my life, who make doing what I do possible.

Thank you to Randy Ladenheim-Gil for the editing.

And finally I want to thank my sister Christy for always lending an ear and my husband Ken for allowing me time to write by taking care of everything else.

Books by Kathi Daley

Come for the murder, stay for the romance.

Zoe Donovan Cozy Mystery:

Halloween Hijinks
The Trouble With Turkeys
Christmas Crazy
Cupid's Curse
Big Bunny Bump-off
Beach Blanket Barbie
Maui Madness
Derby Divas
Haunted Hamlet
Turkeys, Tuxes, and Tabbies
Christmas Cozy
Alaskan Alliance
Matrimony Meltdown
Soul Surrender
Heavenly Honeymoon
Hopscotch Homicide
Ghostly Graveyard
Santa Sleuth
Shamrock Shenanigans
Kitten Kaboodle
Costume Catastrophe
Candy Cane Caper
Holiday Hangover
Easter Escapade
Camp Carter
Trick or Treason
Reindeer Roundup – *December 2017*

Zimmerman Academy The New Normal
Ashton Falls Cozy Cookbook

Tj Jensen Paradise Lake Mysteries by Henery Press

Pumpkins in Paradise
Snowmen in Paradise
Bikinis in Paradise
Christmas in Paradise
Puppies in Paradise
Halloween in Paradise
Treasure in Paradise
Fireworks in Paradise
Beaches in Paradise – *June 2018*
Turkeys in Paradise – *November 2018*

Whales and Tails Cozy Mystery:

Romeow and Juliet
The Mad Catter
Grimm's Furry Tail
Much Ado About Felines
Legend of Tabby Hollow
Cat of Christmas Past
A Tale of Two Tabbies
The Great Catsby
Count Catula
The Cat of Christmas Present
A Winter's Tail
The Taming of the Tabby
Frankencat
The Cat of Christmas Future – *November 2017*

Seacliff High Mystery:

The Secret
The Curse
The Relic
The Conspiracy
The Grudge
The Shadow
The Haunting

Sand and Sea Hawaiian Mystery:

Murder at Dolphin Bay
Murder at Sunrise Beach
Murder at the Witching Hour
Murder at Christmas
Murder at Turtle Cove
Murder at Water's Edge
Murder at Midnight

Writers' Retreat Southern Seashore Mystery:

First Case
Second Look
Third Strike
Fourth Victim
Fifth Night – *January 2018*

A Tess and Tilly Cozy Mystery

The Christmas Letter – *December 2017*

Rescue Alaska Paranormal Mystery
Finding Justice
Finding Answers - 2018

Road to Christmas Romance:
Road to Christmas Past

Chapter 1

Wednesday, December 6

There are people in the world who insist that life is what you make of it. They will tell you that if you work hard enough and persevere long enough, everything you have ever desired will one day be yours. But as I sat in the fifth dingy office I had visited in as many months, and listened as the fifth pencil pusher in a dark suit and sensible shoes looked at me with apologetic eyes, I finally understood that not every dream was realized and not every wish granted.

"Ms. Carson, do you understand what I'm saying?"

I nodded, trying to fight back the tears I absolutely would not shed. "You're saying that you can't consider my grant application unless I've secured a facility."

The man let out a long breath, sounding like a wheeze, which I was sure was more of a sigh of relief. "Exactly. I do love your proposal to build an animal shelter in your hometown, but our grant is designed to be used for ongoing operations. I'm afraid without a physical presence we really must move on."

I leaned over to pick up my eight year old backpack. "Yes. I understand. Thank you so much for your time."

"Perhaps next year?" the man encouraged with a lopsided grin.

I smiled in return. Granted it was a weak little smile that did nothing to conceal my feelings of defeat. "Thank you. I'm certain we'll be able to meet your criteria by the next application cycle."

"We begin a new cycle on June 1. If you can secure a facility by that time, please feel free to reapply," the man encouraged.

I thanked the bureaucrat and exited his office. I tried to ignore the feeling of dread in the pit of my stomach and instead focus on the clickety-clack created as the tile floor came into contact with the two-inch heels I'd bought for just this occasion. Had I really been working on this for more than two years? Maybe it was time to throw in the towel and accept defeat. The idea of building an animal shelter in Rescue, Alaska, was a noble one, but the mountain of fund-raising and paperwork that needed to be scaled in order to make this particular dream come true seemed insurmountable at best.

I dug into my backpack for the cell phone that rang just as I stepped out of the warm building into the bracing cold of the frigid Alaskan winter. I pulled the hood of my heavy parka over my dark hair before wrapping the bulk of my down jacket tightly around my small frame.

"So, how did it go?" My best friend, Chloe Rivers, asked the minute I answered her call.

"It went."

"What happened?" Chloe groaned.

I looked up toward the sky, allowing the snow to land on my face and mask my tears. "The grant is designated for operations, so we aren't eligible until we have a facility. The problem is, we have no money to build a facility and no one will give us a loan for one unless we have capital for operations already lined up. It's an endless cycle I'm afraid we can't conquer."

"We can't give up. You know what you have to do."

"No," I said firmly. "We'll find another way." I knew I sounded harsh, but I had to make Chloe understand.

"Another way?" Chloe screeched. I listened as she took a deep breath before continuing in a softer tone. "Come on, Harmony, you know we've tried everything. There *is* no other way."

Chloe's plea faded as an image flashed into my mind. I closed my eyes and focused on the image before I spoke. I knew from prior experience that it was important to get a lock on the psychic connection before I said or did anything to break the spell. Once I felt I was ready, I opened my eyes and tuned back into Chloe's chatter. I was certain she hadn't missed a beat even though I had missed the whole thing. "Look, I have to go," I interrupted. "Someone's in trouble. I'll call you later."

After hanging up with Chloe, I called a cab and then called Dani Mathews. Dani was a helicopter pilot and one of the members of the search-and-rescue team I belonged to. She'd offered to give me a lift into Anchorage for my meeting today and I'd taken her up on it.

"Someone's in trouble," I said as soon as Dani answered.

"I was about to call you. I just got off the phone with Jake." Jake Cartwright is my boss, my brother-in-law, and the leader of the search-and-rescue team. "There are two boys; one is fifteen and the other is sixteen. They'd been cross-country skiing at the foot of Cougar Mountain. Jake said they have a GPS lock on a phone belonging to one of the teens, so he isn't anticipating a problem with the rescue."

The cab pulled up and I slipped inside. I instructed the driver to head to the airport, then answered Dani. "The boys dropped the phone, so Jake and the others are heading in the wrong direction"

I slipped off my shoes as the cab sped away.

"Do you know where they are?" Dani asked with a sound of panic in her voice.

"In a cave." I closed my eyes and tried to focus on the image in my head. "The cave is shallow, but they're protected from the storm." I took off my heavy parka and pulled a pair of jeans out of my backpack. I cradled the phone to my ear with my shoulder as I slipped the jeans onto my bare legs.

"Where's the cave, Harm?"

I closed my eyes once again and let the image come to me. "I'd say they're about a quarter mile up the mountain."

"Are they okay?" Dani asked.

I took a deep breath and focused my energy. There are times I wanted to run from the images and feelings that threatened to overwhelm and destroy me, but I know embracing the pain and fear is my destiny as well as my burden. "They're both scared, but only one of them is hurt. Call Jake and tell him to check the cave where we found Sitka." I referred to our search-and-rescue dog, who Jake and I found lost on the mountain when he was just a puppy. "And send someone for Moose." I glanced out the window. The snow was getting heavier and it wouldn't be long before we would be forbidden from taking off. "We're almost to the airport. Go ahead and warm up the bird. I should be there in two minutes."

I hung up the phone and placed it on the seat next to me. The driver swerved as I pulled my dress over my head and tossed it aside. I knew the pervert was watching, but I didn't have time to care as I pulled a thermal shirt out of my backpack, over my head, and across my bare chest.

"What's the ETA to the airport?" I demanded from the backseat.

"Less than a minute."

"Go on around to the entrance for private planes. I have the code to get in the gate. My friend is waiting with a helicopter."

As the cab neared the entrance, I pulled on heavy wool socks and tennis shoes. I wished I had my snow boots with me, but the tennis shoes would have to do. The boots were too heavy to carry around all day.

As soon as the cab stopped, I grabbed my phone, tossed some cash onto the front seat, and hopped out, leaving my dress and new heels behind.

"You've forgotten your dress, miss."

"Keep it." I said as I flung my backpack over my shoulder and took off at a full run for the helicopter. As soon as I got in, Dani took off. "Did you get hold of Jake?" I asked as I strapped myself in.

"I spoke to Sarge. He's manning the radio. He promised to keep trying to get through to Jake. The storm is intensifying at a steady rate. We need to find them."

"Moose?"

"Sarge sent someone for him."

I looked out the window as we flew toward Rescue. A feeling of dread settled into the pit of my stomach. The storm was getting stronger, and when a storm blew in without much notice, it caught everyone off guard, so the likelihood of a successful rescue decreased dramatically.

The team I belonged to was one of the best anywhere, our survival record unmatched. Still, I'd learned at an early age that when you're battling Mother Nature, even the best teams occasionally came out on the losing end. I picked up the team radio Dani had tucked into the console of her helicopter. I pressed the handle and hoped it would connect me to someone at the command post.

"Go for Sarge," answered the retired army officer who now worked for Neverland, the bar Jake owned.

"Sarge, it's Harmony. Dani and I are on our way, but we won't get there in time to make a difference. I need you to get a message to Jake."

"The reception is sketchy, but don't you worry your pretty head, Sarge will find a way."

"The boys are beginning to panic. I can feel their absolute horror as the storm strengthens. The one who isn't injured is seriously thinking of leaving his friend and going for help. If he does, neither of them will make it. Jake needs to get there and he needs to get there fast."

"Don't worry. I'll find a way to let Jake know. Can you communicate with the boys?"

I paused and closed my eyes. I tried to connect but wasn't getting through. "I'm trying, but so far I just have a one-way line. Is Jordan there?" Jordan Fairchild was not only a member of the team but she was a doctor who worked for the local hospital.

"She was on duty, but she's on her way."

"Tell her she'll need to treat hypothermia." I paused and closed my eyes again. My instinct was to block the pain and horror I knew I needed to channel. "And anemia. The break to the femur of the injured teen is severe. He's been bleeding for a while." I used the back of my hand to wipe away the steady stream of tears steaking my face. God, it hurt. The pain. The fear. "I'm honestly not sure he'll make it. I can feel his strength fading, but we have to try."

"Okay, Harm, I'll tell her."

"Is Moose there?"

"He will be by the time you get here."

I put down the radio and tried to slow my pounding heart. I'm not sure why I've been cursed with the ability to connect psychically with those who are injured or dying. It isn't that I can feel the pain of everyone who's suffering; it seems to be only those we're meant to help that find their way onto my radar. I'm not entirely sure where the ability came from, but I know when I acquired it.

I grew up in a warm, caring family with two parents and a sister who loved me. When I was thirteen, my parents died in an auto accident a week before Christmas. My sister Val, who had just turned nineteen, dropped out of college, returned to Rescue, Alaska, and took over as my legal guardian. I remember feeling scared and so very alone. I retreated into my mind, cutting ties to most people, except for Val, who became my anchor to the world. When I was fifteen, Val married local bar owner Jake Cartwright. Jake loved Val and treated me like a sister, and after a period of adjustment, we became a family. I began to emerge from my shell. When I was seventeen, Val went out on a rescue. She got lost in the storm, and although the team tried to find her, they came up with nothing but dead ends. I remember sitting at the command post praying harder than I ever had. I wanted so much to have the chance to tell Val how much I loved her. She'd sacrificed so much for me and I wasn't sure she knew how much it really meant.

Things didn't look good, even though the entire team searched around the clock. I could hear them whispering that the odds of finding her alive were decreasing with each hour. I remember wanting to give my life for hers, and suddenly, there she was, in my head. I could feel her pain, but I also felt the prayer in her heart. I knew she was dying, but I could feel her love for me and her fighting to live. I could also feel the life draining from her body with each minute that passed.

I tried to tell the others I knew where she was, but they thought my ramblings were of an emotionally distraught teenager dealing with the fallout of shock and despair. When the team eventually found Val's body exactly where and how I'd told them they would, they began to believe I actually had made a connection with the only family I'd had left in the world.

Of course, the experience of knowing your sister was dying, of feeling her physical and emotional pain as well as her fear as she passed into the next life, was more than a seventeen-year-old could really process. I'm afraid I went just a bit off the deep end. Jake, who had taken over as my guardian, tried to help me, as did everyone else in my life, but there was no comfort in the world that would undo the horror I'd experienced.

And then I met Moose. Moose is a large Maine coon who wandered into Jake's bar, where I worked and lived at the time. The minute I picked up the cantankerous cat and held him to my heart, the trauma I'd been experiencing somehow melted away. I won't go so far as to say Moose has magical powers, at least not any more than I do, but channeling people in life-and-death situations is more draining than I can tolerate, and the only one who can keep me grounded is a fuzzy coon with a cranky disposition.

"Are you okay?" Dani asked as she glanced at me out of the corner of her eye. Her concern for my mental health was evident on her face.

"I'm okay. I'm trying to connect with the boys, but they're too terrified to let me in. It's so hard to feel their pain when you can't offer comfort."

"Can't you shut if off? I can't imagine allowing myself to actually feel and experience what those boys are."

"If I block it, I'll lose them. I have to hang on. Maybe I can get through to one of them. They don't have long."

"Do you really think you have the ability to do that? To establish a two-way communication?"

I put my hand over my heart. It felt like it was breaking. "I think so. I hope so. The elderly man who was buried in the avalanche last spring told me that he knew he was in his final moments and all he could feel was terror. Then I connected and he felt at peace. It was that peace that allowed him to slow his breathing. Jordan said the only reason he was still alive when we found him was because he managed to conserve his oxygen."

"That's amazing."

I shrugged. I supposed I did feel good about that rescue, but I'd been involved in rescues, such as Val's, where the victim I connected with didn't make it. I don't know why it's my lot in life to experience death over and over again, but it seems to be my calling, so I try to embrace it so I'm available for the victims I can save, like the old man last spring.

"The injured one is almost gone," I whispered. "They need to get to him now."

Tears were streaming down my face as I gripped the seat next to me. The pain was excruciating, but I needed to hang on.

Dani reached over and grabbed my hand. "We're almost there. I'm preparing to land. Sarge is waiting with Moose."

Dani guided the helicopter to the ground despite the storm raging around us. As soon as she landed, I opened the door, hopped out, and ran to the car, where Sarge was waiting with Moose. I pulled Moose into my arms and wept into his thick fur. After several minutes, I felt a sense of calm wash over me. I couldn't know for certain, but I felt as if the boy I was channeling had experienced that same calm. I looked at Sarge. "He's gone."

"I'm so sorry, Harm."

"The other one is still alive. He's on the verge of panicking and running out into the storm. Jake and the others have to get to him."

Sarge helped me into the car and we headed toward Neverland, where I knew the fate of the second boy would be revealed before the night was over.

Chapter 2

When I arrived home hours later, I was greeted by a variety of dogs and cats. The second teen had lived, and I let myself feel joy in his survival rather than focusing on the sorrow of the other boy's death. I took a deep breath and hugged Moose to my chest as I let myself into the small house I'd managed to buy with the money I'd inherited when my parents died. Doing what I do, it isn't easy not to focus on the losses, but I know that doing that will only lead to mental instability and an inability to help those I can.

"Hey, guys. Sorry I'm late," I said to the menagerie I lived with after setting Moose onto the hardwood floor. Moose, cranky cat that he is, hissed at Lucy, a mama cat I'd recently rescued. Rescue might not have an animal shelter, but that didn't stop me from trying to save as many animals as I was able to cram into my limited space.

Currently, I share my home with five dogs, four cats, six kittens, eight rabbits, and a blind mule named Homer. Homer, two of the dogs, and the rabbits all live in the barn Jake helped me build, but three of the dogs and all the cats shared the three-bedroom house I called home.

My menagerie began with Moose, who, as I've already shared, wandered into the bar and rescued me from the demons who threatened to destroy me. Shortly after I moved into the house, I found a three-legged dog and named him Lucky. I figured the poor guy might have only three legs, but he was pretty darn lucky he'd been able to avoid me running him over when he veered out in front of my Jeep on a dark, snowy night. During the past three years, other animals had come in and out of my life. Some stayed for the long haul and others were adopted to families who were willing and able to provide a safe, loving home.

After I'd fed the dogs and cats who were housed indoors, I grabbed my rifle and headed outside to care for the animals in the barn. I tilted my head and looked up into the night sky. It was still snowing, and it looked as if the worst of the storm was still ahead of us. I looked back toward the barn and continued on my way.

"Hey, guys," I greeted Kodi and Juno, the two Malamutes I'd adopted after their owner passed away. They'd been working sled dogs when they were younger, but both were past the age when they were able to keep up with the younger dogs. When I'd first adopted the pair, I'd tried to acclimate them to the house, but they'd lived in an outdoor kennel their whole lives with the rest of their team, and outdoors was where they preferred to be.

"I don't have time to take you out for a run, but I'll be home tomorrow, so we'll go for a long snowshoe then. I rescued a skier, and Jake gave me the whole day off to recoup."

The dogs seemed to forgive me for my absence when I added a few treats to their dinner. After cleaning their pen and refilling their water, I fed the rabbits and then headed over to see to Homer's needs. Once everyone was fed, petted, and tucked in, I headed back toward the house. I paused and listened as wolves howled in the distance. The barn was sturdy and I kept it locked at night, but still, I worried the wolves would one day find a way in. The long nights of winter were the most dangerous for domestic animals, as wild prey burrowed in for the winter, leaving the wolves with fewer options.

I looked out toward the edge of the yard, which was bordered by dense woods. The sound of twigs snapping grabbed my attention. I didn't sense there was danger, but I could feel a presence. I cocked my rifle and took several steps in the direction of the noise. Although I carried the rifle for protection, I'd never actually had to shoot an animal. In my experience to date, a shot over the head of a predator was enough to send it on its way. Still, I knew how to hit a target and that one day the target I aimed for could be a wolf or a grizzly who wasn't willing to take no for an answer.

I was about to turn around when I heard a tiny sound. I knelt in the snow with one hand hovering over the rifle just in case, as a small rabbit made its way toward the edge of the forest. I watched as it looked at me and then hopped away. I hoped he'd burrow in for the night so the wolves, who seemed to be getting closer, wouldn't find him. I understood the dynamic in which wolves needed to eat to survive, and I didn't like to think about the beautiful animals starving to death, but I'm such a softie at heart that it pained me to consider the specifics.

I picked up my rifle and continued into the house. My phone rang just as I entered.

"Hey, Chloe. What's up?"

"I'm calling you back about the shelter. I know you don't want to discuss Harley Medford, but you know you have to ask him."

"I can't."

"You can. Let's be honest: It's more that you won't."

"Okay, then I won't." Even as I said the words, my heart constricted in pain as I thought of the strays that littered the town without a haven during the long months of winter. Most winters, more died than lived. I'd saved those I could, but without a shelter to house the rescues, there was only so much I could do.

"I don't know why you're being so stubborn about this. You know he has the resources we need to make the shelter a reality, and given the fact that you two have a history, he might actually do it for you."

"The guy's a famous actor. A *very* famous actor. He's worth tens, maybe even hundreds of millions of dollars. I'm sure he doesn't remember some random girl he used to go to school with a million years ago."

"He may not remember some random girl, but I'm sure he remembers *the kiss*."

I tried not to, but I couldn't keep my own mind from drifting to the memory of that kiss. Harley and I had both been cast in the high school performance of *A Christmas Carol* when I was in the eleventh grade and he was in the twelfth. Harley played Ebenezer Scrooge, while I played Belle, a girl from his past. At the time, being cast as Ebenezer's love interest was the most awesome thing that had ever happened to me. The truth of the matter was, I'd been crushing on Harley for years. During the scene when Belle breaks things off with Ebenezer, we were supposed to hug in a very G-rated way, but somehow, we'd ended up kissing. And what a kiss it was. Every daydream I'd had since that day had centered on that one spectacular kiss. I could still remember the way the world had fallen away and left us isolated in each other's gaze. We stood suspended in time as a stunned auditorium filled with teachers and parents waited for us to continue with our lines. I honestly couldn't remember what it was that broke the spell. Most likely it was Principal Bradford having a coronary over the fact that we'd messed up his perfectly orchestrated play. That one kiss on that magical night had turned out to be the last time I'd seen Harley.

"I'd be willing to bet if Harley's dad hadn't been killed in that accident a few days after the play, and his mom hadn't decided to move away to be near family, you'd have dated the rest of high school and would most likely be married with a couple of kids by now," Chloe continued when I hadn't responded."

"You really are insane." I laughed. "Harley Medford is a superstar. He's dated hundreds of women. In fact, he's probably most famous for the revolving door of women he's slept with. I can absolutely guarantee you that Harmony Carson hasn't been on his radar for a very long time."

"Maybe you're right," Chloe acknowledged. "Maybe he doesn't remember you. But if you want to be assured of raising the money we need for the shelter, someone needs to ask him to participate in our fund-raiser. You're the chairperson for the event, and it should be the chairperson who approaches him. We don't want to look like amateurs."

"We are amateurs," I reminded Chloe.

"Maybe, but we don't want to *look* like amateurs."

I sighed. "I'll think about it. It's been a long day and I'm exhausted. I need to go."

"How was the rescue?"

I felt my heart squeeze as the memory of the pain returned. "We saved one of them. I'll call you tomorrow."

"Okay. If you need to talk, call me."

"Yeah, I will."

I tried to block the pain in my heart as I returned to my chores. Life in Alaska could be challenging. In the part of the state where Rescue was located, the winters were dark and cold and the summers short. A town the size of Rescue didn't have the population to support flashy malls, fast-food establishments, or even a movie theater. If you lived in Rescue, you learned to entertain yourself. I was lucky to have Jake and the others on the search-and-rescue team. We were a family who often hung out in the bar Jake owned and I worked. The residents of Rescue might not have access to the latest film or trendiest fads, but the people who lived and loved here were good folks: hardworking and community-oriented.

Once everyone had been tucked in, I changed my clothes once again and headed into the kitchen. Had I even eaten today? I couldn't remember. I opened cupboards, looking for inspiration, and eventually settled for a peanut butter and jelly sandwich. I poured myself a glass of milk and looked out the window. The storm was intensifying. Lucky came over and sat at my feet. I bent down to pet him and offer comfort. The animals I shared my life with possessed a variety of personalities. Some, like Moose, were prickly and mostly wanted to be left alone, while others, like Lucky, were willing to give and receive love.

The harder the storm blew, the more agitated I became. I rinsed my glass and plate and set them in the sink for a proper washing the following day. I straightened up a bit, checked on Lucy and the kittens, and started a load of laundry, all the while hoping the storm would blow through so I could get some much-needed sleep. Eventually, I pulled on my heavy boots, down jacket, hat, and gloves. I did a final animal check and then headed out to my sixteen-year-old Jeep. I knew it was late and I should go to bed, but I felt restless. Whenever I felt restless, Jake let me bunk with him and Sitka.

I frowned as I looked at the tires that really should have been replaced at the beginning of the winter. I hadn't even noticed that one of them had gone flat. I made okay money working as a waitress at the bar, but feeding five dogs, four cats, six kittens, eight rabbits, and a blind mule was expensive. It seemed no matter how hard I tried, I couldn't seem to set aside enough money for luxuries like tires with actual tread on them. I knew I should try to get a second job, but during the winter there weren't many part-time jobs to be had in places like Rescue.

I looked out at the storm that continued to intensify, changed direction, and headed inside. I'd have to face the demons that threatened to send me running out into the storm alone. I slipped into the long johns I wore to bed, knowing all the while that sleep would elude me. The storm raged outside my window, sending debris into the side of my little house the way it had the nights my parents and Val had died. I turned off the light and pulled Moose to my chest. Moose was an awesome cat who offered comfort during rescues, as seemed to be his job, but he didn't like to be cuddled outside working hours and quickly jumped off the bed, slid onto the floor, and crept underneath. I closed my eyes and let the tears slip through my lids. I knew the storm would pass, as others had before, if only I could make it through the night. Each minute that ticked by seemed like an hour. I tossed and turned, praying for slumber that wouldn't come until I felt the bed give way to a new weight just behind me. I felt a hand slip over my waist and rest across my belly. I gripped the hand that was offered as I finally drifted peacefully into a dreamless sleep.

Chapter 3

Thursday, December 7

When I opened my eyes the next morning, the first thing I saw was Jake, fully clothed and sleeping on top of the covers next to me. It wasn't the first time he'd come to my room or I'd gone to his during a storm, and I was sure it wouldn't be the last. There was nothing hinky going on between the two of us—he was, after all, my father, brother, and boss all rolled into one—but after Val died, I began having nightmares. During those first horrible months, Jake had begun sleeping in my room so he'd be close by if I woke up screaming in the middle of the night. Over time, the nightmares had lessened, only reappearing on the stormiest of nights, and Jake began sleeping in his own room. At least most of the time. Somehow, we both knew there was an open invitation to comfort the other during severe storms. I suspected Jake didn't just come to me to offer comfort, but to receive it as well. I had lost a sister on that horrific night, but Jake had lost a wife.

Jake was snoring deeply, so I grabbed my clothes and headed into the bathroom to change. Chances were, if Jake was asleep in my room, his dog, Sitka, would be sleeping outside the door in the hall. I didn't want to wake Jake, so I bundled up as warmly as I could, grabbed my rifle, and headed out into the frigid morning air to give Sitka and the rest of the household dogs a chance to stretch their legs.

The storm had passed during the night, leaving a blanket of fresh snow that sparkled as the sun made its way up over the horizon. The snow that glistened in the meadow was unmarked except for the small footprints that could only belong to squirrels. I was about to call the dogs back so we could turn around when a yellow Lab came running toward me from beyond the tree line.

"Who do we have here?" I asked the dog, who looked to be both malnourished and pregnant. I knelt down in the snow and ran my hand over her ribs and belly. "You poor thing; we need to get some food in you. Things are a bit crowded back at the house, but we can always make room for one more. Will you come with us?"

The dog didn't answer, but she followed. When we got back to the house, the coffee was made and I could hear Jake in the bathroom. I fed all the animals, including our visitor, before pouring a cup of coffee for myself and heading outdoors to see to the animals in the barn. By the time I returned, Jake was sitting at the table, sipping his coffee and talking to the dog I'd found.

"You should get her in to see Kelly," Jake suggested, referring to Kelly Austin, the local veterinarian. "She's so thin. I hope the pups are okay."

"I'll take her there after we eat. Eggs and bacon okay?"

Jake nodded, and I began preparing breakfast.

"I'll change your tire before I go, but you really need new ones."

I sighed. "I know. Things have been tight."

"I have some used ones in the shed. They're in a lot better shape than the ones you have. I'll take your Jeep and you can use my truck to take the dog to the vet. Come by the bar when you're done and we can trade vehicles."

I knew the used tires in Jake's shed were new ones from the tire center, and I wanted to argue that I could see to my own problems, but I didn't. The truth of the matter was, I needed new tires and I didn't have the money to buy them.

"It looks like there's going to be another storm rolling in this afternoon," Jake said when I didn't respond one way or the other. "I think we should be prepared for the fact that we may be looking at additional rescues. When the morning starts off sunny and beautiful and the storm rolls in unannounced, we always end up with backcountry skiers who aren't prepared."

"I know the drill."

"Are you up for it?"

I paused and looked directly at him. "It doesn't seem I have a choice in these things. Maybe you should plan to close the bar. We'll need the space for the command center."

"I'll also call to remind the radio station to warn folks about the coming storm."

Jake left shortly after we ate and I headed in to take a shower and dress for the day.

******

It was less than three weeks until Christmas, and the general store at the corner of the main street and the highway was covered with so many lights, I was certain it was keeping the astronauts in the International Space Station awake at night. I knew Greta Garbo—yes, that was her real name—would have decorated every surface in the quaint, log cabin–style store, which sold everything from touristy keepsakes to snow boots, hats, and snow shovels, as well as canned food, penny candy, and pharmaceutical supplies. Greta's slogan was, *If you need it, we got it*, and most times she did.

On the opposite corner of the only intersection in town was Chloe's Café, and across the street from that was a hunting, fishing, and camping supply store, Alaskan Outback. Rescue didn't have a wide range of shops from which to choose, but those we did demonstrated authentic Alaskan hospitality.

As the only stoplight in town changed to green, I continued to the far edge of town. After passing the mom-and-pop shops that lined Main Street, I made a left turn toward the lake. The veterinary hospital was usually busy, but the poor dog who had found me looked to need medical attention, so if I had to spend half my day off making certain she got it, that was exactly what I would do.

"Mornin', Justine," I greeted Kelly's receptionist. "Who do we have here?"

"New dog. She found me this morning. She looks to be malnourished and pregnant."

"I'll let Kelly know you're here. I'm sure she can squeeze you in right away." Justine took out a new file folder, which she labeled with my name. She paused. "What are you going to call her?"

I looked at the dog. "What's your name, honey?"

The dog barked.

I looked at Justine. "Honey it is."

Justine laughed and entered her name on the folder. "I'll get her weight and vitals, if you want to follow me back."

I got up and Honey followed me down the hall. The dog was a large animal who should weigh around seventy-five pounds when healthy, but she only came in at fifty-eight. Her temperature was good, so Justine jotted everything down on her chart, then informed me Kelly would be in to see us in just a minute.

I sat on a low bench and Honey sat in front of me on my foot. It was obvious she was nervous in strange surroundings, but she seemed to trust me, and I felt certain as long as we stayed together, she would get through this just fine.

"I see you have another member of your ever-growing family." Kelly smiled as she walked into the room, looking at the chart Justine had just filled out.

"You know me. If there's a need, I find a way. Other than the fact that she needs to be fattened up, Honey seems to be doing okay, though I'm worried about the pups."

Kelly listened to Honey's heart, then lowered the stethoscope to her stomach. "I'd like to do an ultrasound. I think we need to get a look at what's going on inside."

I thought about my empty bank account but nodded. "Yeah, okay. That sounds like a good idea. Can I stay with her?"

"Sure, that'll be fine. Bring her into the back."

The ultrasound showed four puppies, all alive and moving around.

"I'd say she'll drop the pups in the next week, two at the most. I'm going to send some special food home with you, along with feeding instructions. We'll need to supplement Honey's food as long as she's nursing, provided she's able to nurse. I'm also going to send puppy formula home with you, and some bottles for feeding."

I cringed. "I might need to make payments."

"Payments are fine, and I'll tell Justine to give you the friends-and-neighbors discount as well."

"Thanks. I appreciate that."

I followed Kelly out to the reception desk, where she handed Honey's chart to Justine, who gathered all the supplies I'd need, then passed me the bill.

"This can't be right. You do know Honey had an ultrasound, right?"

"It's right. Kelly said to give you the friends-and-neighbors discount."

"But this is 90 percent off."

Justine shrugged. "I don't set the rates; I just do as I'm told. Do you want to take care of this today or should I bill you?"

I looked at the bill again. Even with 90 percent off, I'd need to work a few days to cover the unexpected expense. "Bill me, please."

Justine handed me the paperwork and supplies, along with a coupon for 50 percent off at the feed store. Rescue might be a small town where making a living was difficult at best, but if there was one thing you could say, the locals all took care of one another.

I left the vet's and took Honey home, then gave her the first of the four high-calorie, high-nutrition mini meals she would need each day. Being around to feed her four times a day for an entire week was going to be tricky, but I was determined to make sure she delivered healthy pups, so if I had to turn my life upside down, that was exactly what I'd do.

As I sat and watched Honey dig in to the food, I thought about the animals that were wandering the streets but hadn't been lucky enough to be found by me. Rescue had a lot of strays, and without a shelter to take them to, folks who didn't have the means to care for them usually had to turn a blind eye. "Damn," I said aloud to no one in particular, before picking up the phone and dialing the number Chloe had been pushing on me for the past two weeks.

"Harley Medford," a man with a deep baritone voice answered. I tried not to picture his blue eyes, thick brown hair, and the dimple that appeared every time he smiled.

"Harley, it's Harmony Carson."

My heart pounded as my declaration was met with silence.

"Harmony?" Harley seemed to be as stunned to be hearing from me as I was to have called him. "I was just going to call you."

"You were? Why?"

"You called me, so why don't you tell me what's on your mind first."

"Okay." I took a breath. "I called to speak to you about a fund-raiser I'm heading to benefit the Rescue Animal Shelter."

"Rescue has an animal shelter?"

"Not yet, hence the fund-raiser. Look, I know you're a very busy man, but Chloe Rivers told me that you're in town through Christmas and I hoped you might have some time to help us out. If you don't, I totally understand, but I figured I'd at least ask."

Harley paused before answering, which nearly prompted me to hang up, aborting the ill-fated mission.

"Okay," Harley finally answered. "I'd be happy to help. In fact, I have a warehouse that's sitting empty. It's located just outside of town on a large piece of land, so I think it would work for a shelter."

I put my hand to my heart. "You'd sell it to us?"

"I'd gift it to the town."

I didn't answer right away because I was overwhelmed and didn't know what to say. "Wow. I'm speechless. That would be awesome. If there's anything I can do for you—anything at all—please just ask."

"Actually," Harley said, as if to create a sense of anticipation, "there is something I could use some help with, which leads me to the reason I was about to call you."

I frowned. Uh-oh. "Okay," I said with hesitation. "How can I help you?"

"I guess you heard about Tim Maverick."

"I did." Tim was a fellow alum of Rescue High School. He was in Harley's class, and I remembered them being good friends. I didn't know him well in high school, and while he'd remained in Rescue after graduation, we'd never become friends. I'd heard he'd died of an overdose a couple of weeks before.

"The state troopers declared the cause of death an accidental overdose, but I have reason to believe otherwise," Harley informed me. "I'm in town to look in to the matter and I could really use some help. I have a few ideas as to how to proceed, but I've been gone a long time and don't know all the local players. I asked my sister if she could recommend someone to help, and she gave me your phone number."

I frowned. "Me? Why would she recommend me?"

"It seems you have quite a reputation for finding people, and it just so happens I want someone found."

"Who?"

"The man who killed Tim."

I took a minute and let Harley's words sink in. "So you think he was murdered?"

"I do."

"And do you have a reason to think that?"

"I do. And I'll share that with you, but not over the phone. If you have time, why don't you meet me at the warehouse and I can lay everything out? And just so you know, my offer of donating the warehouse to the town stands, whether you agree to help me or not."

"That's very kind of you."

"Can you meet me there in an hour? You can look over the space, and if you think it'll work, I'll have my attorney take care of the paperwork."

******

I knew before I even looked at it that the building Harley was offering would be prefect. The warehouse had been used for storing materials while the Pipeline was being built. When that was done, it was used to sell snowmobiles for a while, but the lack of new business in Rescue drove the dealership out of business, so it had been sitting empty for years. The building would need to be remodeled on the inside to include separate cat rooms and kennels for dogs, but it was a sturdy building on ten acres, and with a little work, it would be exactly what we'd dreamed of.

Harley's car was parked in front when I arrived. For a brief moment, I seriously considered fleeing, but then I thought of Honey and other dogs like her, took a deep breath, opened the car door, and took a step outside. The wind was blowing and the temperature had dipped to well below zero, so I knew dawdling around outside to avoid going in wasn't the wisest thing to do. I squared my shoulders and headed to the small metal door near the middle of the building, opened it, and stepped inside.

The place really was huge. I thought of the animals we'd be able to save and continued forward to where Harley was pacing and talking on the phone.

"I know what I said, but now I'm telling you I can't make it," Harley argued.

I watched as a look of frustration mingled with irritation crossed his face.

"I'm sorry. I really am, but something's come up and I won't be back until after the first of the year."

I couldn't hear what the person on the other end of the line was saying, but I could see Harley wasn't happy with them.

"No, I can't pop over to Italy for a few days. The movie was your idea. I never wanted to do it. If the fact that I'm delayed is an issue, tell the producer to find someone else."

Harley ran his hand through his hair. He stopped pacing, took a deep breath, and then let it out slowly. "Okay. I understand. See what you can do."

He ended the call, slipped his phone into his pocket, and turned to look at me. His face softened and he grinned. I mean an actual grin, not a polite smile. I wanted to resist, but I couldn't, and grinned back.

"Problems?" I asked.

"My agent. The guy's very ambitious. When I first hooked up with him, I wanted that, but now... Honestly, I'd like to take some time away and just watch it snow."

"I understand. I can't imagine living the type of life you seem to. I'm exhausted just thinking about it."

Harley shrugged. "It's okay. Most of the time." He put his arms out to his side and turned in a full circle. "So, what do you think?"

"It's perfect," I said. "We could not only take care of the domestic animals that end up on the street but eventually expand into helping the local wildlife as well. It's like a dream come true, but are you sure you want to give this building to the town? It has to be worth a fortune."

Harley chuckled. "It really isn't. Not all the way out here. But even if it was, I already have more money than I know what to do with. I'd be honored to give something back to the community where I grew up. I'll even set up a fund to help with the renovations."

"Oh, no. That's too much. I couldn't ask that."

"You didn't ask." Harley stepped forward and took my hand in his. "I want to show you something."

My heart was racing as I let Harley lead me across the empty room. He opened a door I thought would lead to the exterior of the building but instead took us to a finished room the size of a large bedroom.

"This was used by the snowmobile dealer as a business office. It includes a functioning bathroom and is equipped with a pretty decent heater. I figured you could use it as a base of operations during the remodel phase. You may want to build a larger office near the front of the building once you open the place."

I was so overwhelmed with gratitude I didn't know what to say, so I stood on tiptoe and kissed Harley on the cheek. He seemed surprised by my gesture, but after a moment his grin grew even bigger.

"So about…" Harley began and was interrupted by the peal of my phone.

I looked at the caller ID. "It's Jake. I have to take it." I answered the phone and listened. "Okay. I'll be right there." I hung up and then looked at Harley. "There's a rescue underway. They need me. I feel bad about cutting our conversation short, but I have to go."

"No problem. Can I help?"

"Maybe. Do you ski?"

"Black diamond runs since I was a kid."

"You'll need a heavier jacket."

"I have one in the truck."

"Okay. I'm sure Jake will take all the help we can get. We're expecting a busy afternoon. I need to stop to get Moose, but if you don't mind the detour, you can follow me to Neverland."

"Neverland?"

"The bar, not the enchanted land." I turned and headed to the door.

Chapter 4

Twenty minutes later, Harley, Moose, and I arrived at the bar. Jake, as well as two other team members, had already been out when a call came in for a second rescue. By that time the wind was howling and the snow was coming down so hard, it had created whiteout conditions.

"Harley, this is our second-team leader, Wyatt Forester. Wyatt, this is Harley Medford."

"I know who you are, dude." Wyatt slapped Harley on the back.

"Harley has volunteered to help. I figured you could pair him with Landon." I looked around. "Where's Landon?"

"On his way." Wyatt looked at Harley. "You got your own gear?"

"In the truck."

"Get it. It's going to be a long night."

"What do we know?" I asked Wyatt after Harley went back outside.

"Jake, Dani, and Austin are going after a man and his twelve-year-old son. They managed to get a lock on their location before the storm knocked out the cell service, so my feeling is they'll be okay. Just before you arrived, we got a call from a woman staying at the inn who said her sister and her best friend went backcountry skiing this morning and should have been back well before the storm hit. She's been trying to get hold of them but so far hasn't had any luck. We might need you to help out with this one."

"Okay. I'll see what I can do." I sat down at one of the tables Jake had set around the room for small groups to use. I closed my eyes and let my mind relax. After a minute, I wasn't getting anything. "Do we have names for the two missing women?" I asked without opening my eyes.

"Julia and Macy," Wyatt replied.

I focused on the names, willing their location to come to me.

"One blonde and one redhead?" I asked.

"Yes. Do you have them?"

I nodded but still didn't open my eyes. They didn't seem to be injured, but they were cold and scared. I tried to identify where they were, but the area around them was blurred. I concentrated harder, but the connection was weak.

"Were the two women alone?" I asked, eyes still closed.

"As far as I know. The woman who called in the missing persons report didn't mention anyone else."

"I feel someone else. A man." I focused harder. "I sense he's injured. The women feel conflicted. They know they need to return to the inn, but they don't want to leave the man. They're discussing the option of splitting up, but I sense that would put all three of them in danger."

"You need to figure out where they are," Wyatt insisted.

"I'm trying." I focused my mind, trying to block all distractions. "The man is in a great deal of pain. His agony is blocking my ability to concentrate." I put my hand to my chest as my heart began to pound. "Someone else is there."

"A fourth person?" Wyatt asked.

I nodded. "I think so, but I can't get a clear reading." The pain and fear I was picking up were almost unbearable, but I knew I needed to push through the pain if I was going to help the man. "The women are leaving. The man who isn't injured has assured them he'll stay with the injured man while they go for help."

"I guess that makes sense," Wyatt replied.

I sat quietly, focusing on the injured man. I tried to get through to him to offer him comfort, but he was blocking my attempts. He wasn't only in pain; he was scared and angry.

"What do you see now?" Wyatt asked.

"The women have left and the men are alone." I felt Moose jump into my lap as I allowed my attention to settle solely on the injured man. "He's growing weaker. He can't breathe." I began to gasp for air. "The other man is trying to help him, but nothing's working." I put my hands to my own throat.

"Harm, are you okay?" Wyatt asked as he shook me out of my trance. My eyes flew open. Harley, Wyatt, and Landon were all staring at me.

I bowed my head and answered in a quiet voice. "I'm okay. The injured man's gone."

"And the other one?" Wyatt asked.

I took several deep breaths, then closed my eyes. I shook my head. "I'm no longer sensing him." I opened my eyes. "Call the inn. Tell the woman who made the call that her sister and friend are on their way back. Have them call us. We'll need a location so we can retrieve the body of the man who died."

Wyatt went to make the call, Landon left to speak to Sarge, and Harley sat down at the table with me. I picked up Moose and snuggled him close. I knew the night wasn't over and felt the need to recharge my emotions.

"Can I get you anything?" Harley asked.

I shook my head. "I'm okay." I set Moose on the floor. "I'm going to go wash my face. Tell Wyatt I'll be right back."

I headed to the ladies' room, where I'd have a few minutes to myself. In many ways, I'd become accustomed to the emotional turmoil the connections put my mind and body through, but there were times they felt as raw and heart-wrenching as the very first time. Losing a stranger was nothing like feeling Val's life force fade away, but the part of me that was a friend, sister, and child knew that for someone, their life would never be the same.

I splashed water on my face and dried it with a paper towel before I went back out to the bar. Harley handed me a cup of coffee and I smiled as I accepted it. He sat down at the table and waited quietly while I sipped the hot brew he'd provided.

"What was that all about?" Harley asked.

"I'm able to connect with people I'm meant to help."

"Connect?"

"I can see them and feel their physical and emotional pain. Once I'm able to make a connection, I can usually get a pretty good read on where they are and what sort of help they need."

"Is it always so intense?" he eventually asked.

"Not always, but yeah, a lot of the time. Unfortunately, a lot of people lose their lives out there on that mountain. No one ever thinks it's going to be them or someone they love until it is."

"I remember hearing about skiers who lost their way in a storm when I was a kid. You'd think people would understand how dangerous going out without a guide can be."

I took another sip of my coffee. "It seems to be human nature to think that bad things happen to other people."

"How long have you been able to do this? Sense other people?"

"Since I was seventeen."

Harley put his hand on mine. "I can't even begin to comprehend dealing with the trauma you seem to be able to connect with. You're a very special woman."

"Special, no. Cursed, maybe."

Harley looked as if he was going to argue with me when Wyatt interrupted. "Jake's on the radio for you." He handed me the receiver.

"Hey, Jake, what's up?"

"We have the man and his son we were after, but they said they saw two skiers heading up the mountain when they were coming down. We're going to come in with the two we have, but if you sense anything, or if someone calls in a missing persons report, let me know."

"Okay, I will."

"Is Jordan still there?" Jake asked.

"Wyatt said she was called in to work."

"Okay. Ten-four."

I set the radio down and looked at Harley. "In case you were wondering, Jordan is a team member and also a doctor."

"How many are on the team?"

"There are eight of us, including Sarge, who usually mans the radio. Jake Cartwright is the leader of the pack and Austin Boswell, a local firefighter, is our newest recruit. Landon Stanford is the brains of the team, and Wyatt makes sure we stay on track and has serious mountain-climbing skills."

"And the others?"

"Dani Mathews owns a helicopter and helps out when air rescue is required and, as I said, Jordan's a doctor. If the rescue warrants it, we have a handful of others who help out too."

"It seems you all work well together."

I nodded. "We're a family. We all have unique talents we bring to the table and support one another no matter what."

A look of longing crossed Harley's face.

"Are you close to the people you work with?" I asked.

Harley shook his head. "No. Not really."

"But you have friends back home."

Harley shrugged. "Sure, I guess. I travel a lot, so it's hard to establish meaningful relationships. If I stop to think about it, the only one I'm really close to is my sister Polly."

"I haven't talked to Polly in ages. Is she still living in Los Angeles?"

"For now. She's dating Mike Stinson, and it seems to be getting pretty serious."

"Rescue's Mike Stinson?" Mike was a local doctor who'd just gotten back from two years with Doctors Without Borders."

"Polly got her degree in nursing and did a stint with Doctors Without Borders. She happened to be assigned to the same team as Mike. They remembered each other from when Polly and I lived here. Now that Mike is back in Rescue, I expect an engagement is on the horizon."

"Is Polly here? In Rescue?"

"No. She's still in LA. She's committed to the hospital where she works for to finish out the year, but she's a free agent as of January."

"It would be awesome if she came back here. I always liked her. Do you think Mike and Polly plan to settle here?"

Harley shrugged. "I'm not sure. They have ties to Rescue, but they both have a bit of wanderlust as well. I wouldn't be at all surprised if they don't get hitched and then set off on another adventure."

"I can understand that. Sometimes I think it would be fun to see the world, but in the end, I'm just a homebody. I think I'd be homesick after only a week or two, if I ever did decide to leave Rescue."

"So you've been here this whole time? Since we were in school together?"

I nodded.

"College?"

I shook my head. "I didn't have a burning passion to do anything different with my life than I'm doing right now, so I didn't see the need to spend all that money. I do like to learn about new things, so I read a lot. Pretty much everything you can learn in college you can learn from a book."

"I guess." Harley took another sip of his coffee. "It seems like things have quieted down. How long do you need to stay?"

"As long as it takes. I hope I'm wrong, but I'm afraid we're just getting started."

Unfortunately, I was right. Not five minutes later, an image flashed through my mind. A child. God, I hated it when children were involved. I closed my eyes and tried to make a connection. I could sense her fear. She was cold but not injured.

"Wyatt," I called without opening my eyes.

"I'm here, babe. What do you have?"

"A young girl. Maybe six or seven. She's in a dark space. It's very small."

"A cave?" Wyatt asked.

I focused my energy. "No. Not a cave. A pipe of some sort."

"A drainage pipe?" Wyatt asked.

I took several deep breaths and sat quietly. "I'm not sure. Maybe. She's cold. So very cold." I felt myself begin to shiver. "She wants to get out, but she can't. She's stuck." I frowned as I focused in. "She isn't in pain, but she can't move her foot. Her left foot."

"Where is she, babe?" Wyatt asked. "We need a location."

"I know." Tears began to stream down my face. "The girl's becoming hysterical. She's trying to move her foot, but it's trapped by something. She's calling for her mother."

I felt the fingers of someone's hand thread through mine and squeeze. I still hadn't opened my eyes, but I knew it was Harley.

"There's water," I gasped. "And it's cold. So cold."

"It has to be a drainage pipe leading from the mountain into the lake," Wyatt said.

"I don't think so. It's snowing, not raining. I think it's more of a spill drain carrying water from the lake."

"Okay, but it's a big lake. Where do we look?"

I focused as hard as I could, blocking out the world around me as well as Harley's distracting hand. "I hear something. A creaking. It sounds like something blowing back and forth in the wind." I tried harder. The groan sounded familiar. I knew I'd heard it before.

My eyes popped open. "Swings. The sound is coming from swings. Check the playground down by the lake."

Landon walked in just then, and he went with Wyatt, leaving Harley and me alone.

"Are you okay?" Harley used a finger to wipe a tear from my cheek.

Moose climbed into my lap and I hugged him to my chest. "I'm all right."

My heartbeat slowed as Moose purred in my ear. Harley went into the kitchen to grab me another cup of coffee just before Jake, Dani, and Austin walked in.

"Did you get the man and his son back in one piece?" I asked.

"We did. They were cold but fine. I dropped them at the hospital as a precaution. Did the two women make it back okay?" Jake answered.

"The woman who called in the report is going to call when they arrive. The man they were with died, so we'll have a retrieval when the storm lets up."

"Damn," Jake said before taking a deep breath and blowing it out. "I heard the call about the little girl. Should we head out to assist?"

I paused and closed my eyes. "No, they have her."

Harley returned with my coffee and set it down on the table.

"I heard you were in town." Jake slapped Harley on the back. "It's good to see you, man."

"Good to see you too." Harley put his hand on Jake's shoulder. "Been a while."

"Too long."

I should have realized Jake and Harley knew each other; Jake had lived in Rescue back before Harley left. I set Moose back in his chair, then headed to the ladies' room while the guys caught up. I wasn't picking up anything at the moment, but my instinct told me the night wasn't over and I needed to stay alert. I splashed water on my face, then looked in my reflection in the mirror. Dark hair, a few freckles, average features that weren't likely to turn anyone's head. I read the tabloids and knew the kind of women Harley was linked to: models, actors, singers, all beautiful and all a whole lot more exciting than I'd ever be.

By the time I returned to the table I felt refreshed. There was a fresh cup of coffee waiting for me, so I sat down across from Harley. "It looks like there's a break in the action. Why don't you tell me what you're hoping I can do for you?"

He pulled a photo out of his pocket and handed it to me. It featured a tall man with dark hair wearing a heavy parka and sunglasses.

"What am I looking at?" I asked.

"About a month ago, I got an envelope in the mail from Tim. We were really close in high school but hadn't stayed in touch since I left Rescue other than a Christmas card and a chatty note every year. Then, last summer, I ran into him at the wedding of a mutual friend. Tim seemed to have gotten his act together and was in a good place. We talked about getting together over the Christmas holiday, so I wasn't surprised to hear from him. But the envelope didn't contain an invitation to get together, just this photo, along with a note saying he'd gotten himself into a whole heap of trouble and wasn't sure how things were going to work out. He said he had a plan to fix things, but if it didn't work out and he were to meet an untimely death, chances were this man had probably killed him."

I frowned. "Do you know who this is?"

Harley shook his head. "I have no idea. I'm in Rescue to find out. I've already asked around a bit, but no one will admit to knowing the guy. I'm not even sure he's still, or ever was, here. Tim had a knack for getting himself in and out of trouble, and I know he used drugs in the past, but given the timing of his overdose and the envelope he sent me, I think his death may not have been an accident."

I narrowed my gaze. "It does seem like too much of a coincidence to actually be one."

"I feel like I need to track down this man. Either he killed Tim or he knows who did. Can you help me?"

I paused. "I don't know if I can find him, but I'm willing to try. The first thing we need to do is figure out who he is. Landon is a genius on the computer. If it's okay with you, I'd like to bring him in on this. He might be able to use facial recognition software to identify the man. Do you know if there was any sort of investigation when Tim died?"

Harley shook his head. "As far as I can tell, no. His body was found in a ravine just outside of town. He died of a heroin overdose. There were track marks on his arm and an empty syringe near his body. As I said, Tim had a drug problem when he was younger, but he's been clean for years. Besides, even when he was using, he wasn't doing heavy-duty drugs like heroin."

I looked at the photo again. "Okay. I'll help you, but I can't make any promises. Let's bring Landon and Jake in on this. They might be able to help."

"'Bring Landon and Jake in' on what?" Wyatt asked, walking up behind me.

"Grab them and we'll fill you in."

Chapter 5

Friday, December 8

Landon and Jake agreed to help find out what had happened to Tim. Landon cleaned up the photo Harley had received in the mail and was running the facial recognition program, and Jake knew where Tim had been living, so he was meeting Harley and me the next morning to look around.

The cabin Tim lived in was about ten miles from the commercial area of Rescue. It was small, with a single bedroom, a small bathroom, and a living area that incorporated a seating area and a functional but tiny kitchen. The first thing I noticed when I went inside was that the place had been tossed. Every drawer was upended, the sofa cushions were slashed, and the contents of every cupboard had been emptied onto the floor.

"Wow," I said as I took it all in.

"Wow is right," Jake agreed. He turned to look at Harley. "Did Tim say anything about having possession of something that someone else might have been after?"

Harley looked as shocked as I felt. "No. The envelope I received contained the photo and a very short note stating that if something happened to him, it most likely wasn't an accident."

"Do you have the note?" Jake asked.

"Back at the inn."

"We'll stop by to look at it when we're done here." Jake looked at me. "For now, let's just look around and see what we find."

"What are we looking for?" I asked.

Jake shook his head. "I don't know. I'm hoping if we see it, we'll know it."

By unvoiced agreement, the three of us split up and searched different sections of the cabin. It seemed odd to me that virtually all the breakable objects in the place had been shattered. Did whoever broke in think Tim had hidden whatever it was they were after inside something? If that were true, whatever we were looking for would have to be small. How small I didn't know because I had absolutely no idea what could have gotten Tim killed.

"I don't know how we're ever going to find anything in this mess, especially because we don't know what we're looking for," I said aloud after we'd been searching the place for nearly thirty minutes.

"It does seem pretty pointless," Harley agreed. "I guess I should have made more of an effort to follow up with Tim."

"Did you speak to him at all after receiving the letter?" I asked.

Harley hung his head before answering. "No. I called him right after I got it, but he didn't pick up the call. I left a message and asked him to call me back, but he didn't. I should have been more diligent, but I was in the middle of wrapping a movie that was already behind schedule and the letter slipped my mind. The next thing I knew, I got a call from my sister, letting me know Tim was dead. I've been beating myself up about it ever since. I should have realized Tim was in real trouble and done more to help him when I had the chance."

"You couldn't have known he'd fallen off the wagon," I reasoned.

"I don't think he had," Jake countered. "If Tim had been using, there would be signs, and there isn't anything in here to indicate that he was. I haven't found a single bottle of alcohol, any pills, or even a prescription; not a syringe, not a bong, nothing."

"That's a good point," I realized. "What are the chances Tim would be clean all this time and then suddenly decide to crawl into a ditch and overdose? If he was back to his old ways, I'm sure we would find evidence. He lived alone, so he wouldn't have reason to hide if he was using again."

"Which makes me feel even worse." Harley sighed. "Of all the people he knew, he chose to reach out to me for help, and I let him down."

"Why do you think he did reach out to you?" I asked. "You're a busy man who didn't live anywhere near him. Why do you think he sent the letter to you instead of someone closer? Someone he saw on a regular basis? And if he did think the man in the photo was going to kill him, why didn't he say who he was in the letter?"

"I don't know," Harley said, frustration evident in his voice. "I don't think there's anything here. If whatever Tim had that got him killed was in the cabin, whoever broke in most likely has it. And if Tim hid it somewhere else, I don't see any clues that would lead to it."

I sighed. "It's not looking good. If we knew what we were looking for, then maybe…"

"Let's head over to the inn and look at the letter he sent you," Jake said. "After that, I need to get to the bar. It'll be busy with the weekend crowd."

******

The Moosehead Inn was owned and operated by a very nice couple, Marty and Mary Miller. They'd moved to Rescue after leaving the big city to seek a simpler way of life, and both seemed to have adjusted to the Alaskan lifestyle quite well. Marty owned a sled dog team he entered in regional competitions, and Mary belonged to several women's groups in addition to cooking for and seeing to her guests. The first thing I always noticed when entering the inn was the delightful smell of something baking in the oven. Harley went up to his room with Jake while I wandered into the kitchen to have a chat with Mary.

"Gingerbread?" I asked when I found Mary using the electric mixer.

"Harmony," Mary said, turning off the mixer and wiping her hands on a rag. "I'm sorry. I didn't hear you come in."

"That's okay. Jake's here with Harley to find something in his room, so I decided to stop in to say hi."

"It's been such a thrill to have a big name like Harley Medford staying at our little inn. When he first called about a reservation I thought he'd be difficult to get along with, being such a star and all, but as it turns out, he's as pleasant as he is good-looking."

"Harley's always been nice. I was happy to see Hollywood hadn't changed that. He's even donating a warehouse for us to use as an animal shelter."

"He mentioned that. Such a generous gift, although I suppose he can afford it. Would you like a cup of coffee and a piece of ginger cake?"

"I don't have long."

"I'll send some cake with you," Mary offered. "I know Harley's fond of the cake and I seem to remember gingerbread is one of Jake's favorites as well."

"Thank you. That would be very nice."

"So, what are you young people up to?" Mary asked as she sliced three pieces of cake and transferred them into a plastic container.

"Jake and I are helping Harley with a project."

"Harley's been asking around about Tim Maverick's death. I do hope he finds out what happened. Tim sometimes helped out at the church. He was such a nice young man. Didn't always use the sense God gave him, but I can't believe he was back on drugs again. He seemed to have turned a corner, if you know what I mean."

"I do. Tim and I didn't run into each other often—probably because I spend most of my time in a bar and he was a recovering addict—but the few times I saw him, he seemed alert and happy. Harley thinks he might not have taken the drugs voluntarily, and I have to say I agree."

"I do hope you can find out what happened to that poor boy."

Tim had been thirty, so not really a boy, but Mary was at least in her fifties, so I imagined it was all relative.

"Can you think of anyone we can talk to? Maybe someone Tim hung out with who might know what had been going on in his life in the weeks leading up to his death?"

Mary paused. "I suppose you should speak to Jared Martin. They seemed pretty close. And I noticed Tim with his eye on Teresa Toller at services. I think they might have been sweet on each other."

"Thanks. I'll speak to them."

Mary handed me the plastic container with the cake inside just as Jake and Harley came downstairs to the main floor of the inn.

"What's next?" I asked them.

"I need to call my agent," Harley answered. "He's left twenty messages in the past two hours. I'm assuming we need to do some negotiating on the Italy project. Can I meet you later? Maybe for dinner?"

I glanced at Jake.

"Fine with me," he answered. "You have the night off. I'll take you to get your Jeep."

"Thanks." I held up the plastic container. "Mary sent cake."

"Then I'll have some of that when I drop you."

I said good-bye to Mary and Harley and followed Jake out into the cold Alaskan day. "Did you find anything interesting in the letter?" I asked.

"No. It was just as Harley said: a few sentences stating he felt he was in danger and that the man in the photo might kill him."

"I wonder why Tim didn't go to the authorities."

"I guess he didn't feel he could trust them. I hope we can help Harley find his answers, but I have to be honest: It's a long shot. We don't even know who the man in the photo is, or when he was in Rescue."

I opened the container, tore off a corner of one of the pieces of cake, and popped it in my mouth. I hadn't taken time for breakfast and I was starving. "It does seem like we're up against a brick wall. I thought I'd talk to a few people this afternoon, show the photo around, and see if anyone has seen the man. Last I knew Landon had the photo, so I'll stop by his place to pick it up."

I checked on all my animals and let the dogs out for a quick run before I headed to Landon's. He'd already scanned it into his computer and was seeking a match from his facial recognition database. It was another long shot the man would even be in the database, but eliminating that possibility seemed the best place to start.

I picked up the photo and headed to the pharmacy, which Tim's friend, Jared Martin, ran. He was a recent transplant to Rescue, having moved here only two years before. In a way, it seemed odd that Jared, who was steady and serious and had an advanced degree, would be friends with Tim, who, even after he got sober, was spontaneous and irresponsible and tended to get into difficult, complicated situations. Still, Tim was friendly and outgoing, and he'd always had a joke to tell and a smile on his face, so I imagine that for Jared, who lived a serious life, he was a nice change of pace.

"Afternoon, Harmony. What can I help you with today?" Jared asked.

"Information," I answered. "Information about Tim Maverick, to be precise."

Jared bowed his head. "I still can't believe he's gone. It doesn't make any sense."

"I guess you heard Harley Medford is in town."

"Everyone's heard Harley Medford is in town. The guy's the biggest thing to come to Rescue in, well, forever."

"I'm not sure if you know this, but Harley grew up here. In fact, he and Tim were best friends all through high school."

"You don't say."

"Harley, understandably, is upset about Tim's passing and is looking in to the details surrounding his death. He's of the opinion Tim hadn't fallen off the wagon and wouldn't voluntarily shoot up."

"I agree, to a point. Right before his death, Tim seemed distracted, even somewhat depressed. He never would tell me what was on his mind, but I wasn't totally surprised when he chose to end his own life."

"So you think he intentionally overdosed?"

"That would be my guess, although I suppose an accidental overdose is equally as likely."

"Do you recognize this man?"

Jared took the photo I held out. "No. Who is he?"

"I'm not sure, but it seems to be someone Tim was in some way involved with. Did he say anything to you that would lead you to believe he had a project he was working on before he died?"

Jared pursed his lips, then shook his head. "Not really. He did say he'd gotten a part-time job. He didn't tell me who he was working for, but it sounded like he was a courier of some sort."

"A courier?"

Jared shrugged. "I didn't dig for details. You know how Tim could be. Once you got him off on a tangent, he could talk your ear off."

"Can you think of anyone with whom he may have shared the details of his job?"

Jared put his hand on his chin as he thought about it. "I suppose you could have a chat with Gill Greenland. I don't know for certain he spoke to Tim, but Gill usually chats with his customers while he's filling them up, and if he caught Tim on the right day, he might have discussed what he was up to."

"Thanks. I'll head over there now. If you think of anything later that seems like it could be important, will you call me?"

"Sure thing. I hope you figure this out."

The gas station Gill owned was only a few blocks away and I needed gas anyway, so I pulled up to the pump. Gill seemed distracted as he looked up into the sky, which was dark and heavy, and the temperature had come up a bit, so I thought we were in for another storm.

"Storms coming," he said when I rolled down my window.

"Yeah, it looks that way."

"Fill 'er up?"

"Please," I said and stepped out of the vehicle.

"Could be the first of many. Heard we're in for another series of strong storms."

"Hopefully, there'll be enough warning with this one, so we won't have skiers trapped out in the storm like we do when things blow in real fast."

"Yeah, that'd be nice, but the people who come up here to ski don't seem to bring the common sense

God gave them with them. It's not right we have to put our own folks in danger to rescue them."

I tucked my hands into my jacket pockets for added warmth as the wind began to pick up. "I guess you heard Harley Medford donated a warehouse for us to use as an animal shelter."

"Yup, I heard. That was right nice of him."

"It was." I nodded. "In return for his generous donation, I'm helping him look in to the specifics surrounding Tim Maverick's death."

Gill pulled the gas nozzle from my Jeep and returned it to the pump. "I remember Harley and Tim were friends. It was a real shame what happened to Tim. A real shame indeed."

"Had you spoken to Tim in the weeks before he died?"

"Sure. Tim came in for a top off a couple of times a week. We'd chat for a minute while I pumped the gas."

"How did he seem?"

"Seem?"

"The official cause of death was a heroin overdose. Did Tim seem stressed or distracted to you? Did it seem as if he may have been using again?"

Gill looked up and rolled his eyes back, as if searching for the information I required. "He did seem like he had something heavy on his mind the last time I saw him. He was in a hurry, more so than usual, and his tank was nearly empty, even though I'd just filled it up the day before."

"Did he say where he'd driven?"

Gill shook his head. "Nope. It seemed as if he might have been leaving town again, though. He asked about the road conditions on the highway north of here."

I said a brief, silent prayer the charge would go through and handed Gill my credit card. "Did it seem as if he'd been drinking or using drugs?'

Gill handed me back my card, along with a receipt to sign. "No. Just sort of skittish, if you know what I mean. He kept looking around, like he had his eyes open for someone or something."

I took the photo out of my pocket. "Do you recognize this man?"

"No, I can't say I do. Is it someone I should know?"

"Not necessarily. I just have reason to believe he's someone Tim was connected to prior to his death."

I thanked Gill for the conversation and climbed back into my Jeep. I still wanted to speak to Teresa Toller, but I needed to get home to see to the animals before my dinner with Harley, so I made a note to follow up with her the next day.

Chapter 6

The storm Gill had predicted had blown in with force, so Harley and I decided to just have dinner at Neverland. Even though he'd grown up in Rescue, he lived in Los Angeles now and wasn't used to driving in the snow, so I volunteered to pick him up rather than the other way around. Even before this storm it had been snowing on and off, and many of the roads in town hadn't been recently plowed, but thanks to the studded snow tires Jake had given me, I figured I'd be fine as long as I avoided the really deep drifts.

"Okay, guys, I won't be gone long. Please don't destroy the house while I'm away." I looked at the husky pup who had found her way into my shed a few months back. "That means you, Shia. I still haven't sewn up the pillow you tore up the last time I left you in the house while I went out. This is your last chance to prove you can respect my space, or next time you'll find yourself in the barn."

Shia didn't really mind the barn, and I left her there when I was going to be out for long periods of time, but she was a young and beautiful dog I knew could easily find a forever home if she'd just learn some manners. We'd been working on eliminating certain behaviors and she seemed to have made progress, at least when I was at home, but the only way to test her ability to behave while I was away was to leave her alone in the house for short periods of time to see how it went.

Harley was waiting for me when I pulled up in front of the inn and came out to the Jeep without my having to go in to get him. Marty had strung colored lights around the windows and along the roofline of the three-story structure, which gave the place a warm, Christmassy feel.

"It's really coming down," Harley said as he climbed into the passenger seat.

"Yeah. We've had a system of strong storms coming through as of late. They're predicting several feet of new snow over the next few days."

"I forgot how relentless the winters can be up here. Still, I prefer it to the heat in LA at this time of the year."

"Christmas and snow do go together. How'd your talk with your agent go?"

Harley sighed. "It looks like I have no choice but to go to Italy, as he promised on my behalf. I leave tomorrow, but I should be back before Christmas."

"I'm sorry to hear that," I said as I pulled into the parking lot at Neverland.

"Proving that Tim's death wasn't an accident and then finding his killer is important to me, so the timing couldn't be worse. I tried everything I could to get out of it, but my agent insists I'm obligated to follow though. I did speak to my attorney, though, and he's drawing up the paperwork to have the warehouse deeded to the town. And I set up a fund at the local bank that can be used to buy supplies and pay for labor for the remodel. It's fine with me if you want to go ahead and get started right away."

I opened my door and slid out of the Jeep. "Again, thank you so much. The town and the animals of Rescue are extremely grateful."

"I'm more than happy to help." Harley took my arm and we hurried to the front door of the bar. Once inside, we chose a table near a window. Jake brought us a pitcher of beer while Harley looked at the menu. Once he'd decided, we gave Jake our order.

"So, the movie in Italy…is it an action flick?" Harley wasn't only famous for action films, but he often did his own stunts.

"It's an indie film that's more of a coming-of-age sort of thing. Thankfully, I only have a small part that shouldn't take long to film. I tried to talk my agent out of agreeing that I'd participate at all, but the producer wanted to use my name as a marketing ploy even though I'm only in a few scenes. It feels sort of dishonest to me to promote it as one of my films, but it's done all the time. I might have fought harder against doing it, but my agent and the producer are old friends, so I let them talk me into it."

"Well, I hope it'll go smoothly and you'll be able to get back to Rescue in plenty of time for the holidays."

"Hopefully. I already told my agent I'm taking some time off next year. I've been doing one movie after another for so long, I've forgotten what else life has to offer."

I watched as Harley took a sip of his beer. He did look tired, but I supposed he might not have been sleeping well since finding out what happened to Tim.

"I'm sure you're asked this all the time, but why did you decide to go into acting in the first place?"

"I didn't really choose acting; it sort of chose me. After my dad died, my mom moved us to Los Angles to be near her family. I was halfway through senior year of high school, and I'll admit the move on top of my dad's death was hard on me. I joined a gym and began working out to deal with my life. I got in to Parkour, and after a few months I decided to enter some competitions. I was participating in one when a guy came up to me and asked if I'd ever considered being a stuntman. It had never occurred to me, but I was feeling pretty unfocused, so I agreed to meet him to explore the idea. One thing led to another, and I got a few gigs. I was doing a movie and one of the stars got hurt. They asked me to stand in for him until they could find a replacement. The next thing I knew, I was signing a contract to take over the role."

"Wow. That's amazing. Considering you're now one of the biggest action stars in the world, I'm assuming you did well in your first role."

Harley shrugged. "Apparently. So, what about you? What have you been up to since we shared the stage all those years ago?"

"Maybe you remember my parents died in an accident and I was living with Jake and my sister, Val. About a year after your father's death, Val was killed in a rescue. Jake took over as my guardian and I started helping out in the bar. I worked in the kitchen until I turned twenty-one, then switched to tending bar and waiting on tables. I won't say being a bartender was my dream job, but the tips are pretty good and I like spending time here with Jake and the gang."

"It's obvious you're all really close."

I nodded. "Like I said, we're a family."

"Have you ever thought of trying something else?"

I lifted one shoulder. "Sometimes I play with the idea, but Rescue is my home, and there aren't a lot of career opportunities here. I'm very involved with the search-and-rescue team, and working for Jake gives me the flexibility I need to participate in every rescue. How about you? Do you ever think of doing something other than acting?"

"Lately, all the time."

I was surprised to hear that. Harley was very good at what he did. "Is there something else you're interested in?"

"Not specifically, but there are times I think about spending my life doing something that makes a real difference, rather than playing the part of characters who make a difference. Acting has been good to me, but I'm not sure I want to do it for the rest of my life."

"I can understand that."

Sarge came over with our food and we paused the conversation. Sarge had been a cook in the army and now he did most of the cooking here. He might have a rough and gruff exterior, but he was a genius in the kitchen.

"This looks really good," Harley said as he cut into his steak.

"Sarge is an excellent cook. I think you'll enjoy everything he makes."

Harley and I spent the next few minutes eating rather than talking. As usual, Sarge's five-cheese lasagna was delicious, as was his homemade bread fresh from the oven. I was buttering my second slice when Teresa Toller walked in with Greta Garbo. They took a seat near the door.

"See the two women who just walked in?" I whispered.

Harley turned and looked in the direction of the front of the bar. "Yeah. What about them?"

"The younger of the two was a friend of Tim's. Her name's Teresa. I'd planned to speak to her tomorrow, but I think I'll scoot over there and say hi after they order."

"Do you think she knows anything?"

I tilted my head. "Hard to know, but it never hurts to ask. Teresa is quiet and sort of shy. I'm not sure she'll share what she knows if we both approach her. I think it will be best if I go over alone."

"Whatever you think is best. Just give me a wave if you need me."

I waited a few minutes, then made my way over to Teresa's table. I greeted both women, then asked if they'd be willing to answer a couple of questions. Greta noticed Harley and started to make noise about an autograph. I didn't want to call all that much attention to Harley and me, so I assured her he'd be spending some time in town and would most likely stop by her store at some point. She could ask him for an autograph when he came in.

Teresa told me what she knew and I went back to Harley.

"So? Did she tell you anything?" he asked.

"Yes and no. She didn't know who the man in the photo was, but she did say Tim had taken a job as a courier that required him to be out of town several times a month. He was vague about where he went and declined to say what he was transporting, but he'd pick up an item from one location and deliver it to another. Given the fact he only worked a few days a month, she thought he was making a lot of money. That concerned her, because she could only imagine he'd gotten involved in something illegal, but Tim assured her what he was doing was on the up and up."

Harley furrowed his brow. "He told me he had a job as a courier, but he didn't say he only worked a few days a month. If he was paid well for just a few days' work, he probably *was* transporting something illegal."

"Maybe he didn't realize that at first. Maybe once he figured it out, he was too far in to get out. Maybe that's why he's dead."

"Makes sense. Did Teresa have any other information? A name, or maybe a clue as to where Tim went when he was away?"

"She said he was very careful not to give away any specifics. She did say that in the weeks before his death he seemed nervous. She asked him what was going on, but he wouldn't tell her anything. He left for one of his jobs several days before he was found dead."

Harley's face grew hard. "He must have been working for the man in the photo. Tim must have had second thoughts, so he killed him. We have to find him and make him pay for what he did to Tim."

I placed my hand over Harley's. "We will."

Chapter 7

Friday, December 15

"So, are you guys ready to head back?" I asked the handful of dogs I'd taken for a snowshoe a week after my dinner with Harley. He'd left the following morning for Italy and I'd continued to ask around about the man in the photo and Tim's last weeks on earth. Most everyone agreed Tim had been doing well and there'd been no sign he'd fallen off the wagon. They also agreed he'd seemed to have something on his mind, but no one knew who the man in the photo was. I'd spoken to a lot of people, yet I felt I didn't know anything more now than I did from the start.

Shia ran over to me and I turned to look back at Lucky. He tended to have a hard time in the deep snow, so I pulled a sled he didn't mind riding on. The others lumbered along at their own pace, some walking behind me in my tracks, others running ahead and returning again and again. I'd left Honey at home because she was about to drop her pups at any minute and I didn't want it to happen a mile or more from home.

I had the night off and planned to head home, heat up a can of soup, and maybe read one of the books I'd been meaning to get to. It wasn't often I found myself with absolutely nothing I had to do and I found I rather liked it. Of course, what I *should* do was wrap the small stack of presents I'd purchased for Jake and the gang, and I still hadn't gotten around to cutting a tree for the living room. I considered doing that, but it was getting cold and the sun was already low in the sky, so the tree would have to wait for another day.

I also needed to spend some time at the shelter on Saturday. As he'd said he would before he left for Italy, Harley had drawn up papers deeding the warehouse to the town for use as an animal shelter, and the remodel of the interior had begun. The addition of outdoor runs and play areas would need to wait until the snow melted next summer, but with any luck the entire project would be complete and we'd be open for business well before the following winter's snows arrived.

When I returned to the house I found a man with long blond hair, big brown eyes, a deep golden tan, and a body only a true athlete could hone, sitting on my sofa with a Border collie sitting next to him and Honey half on his lap.

"Who are you?" I asked as I leaned my rifle against the wall so I could slip out of my backpack, all the while trying to figure out if I'd met the man at some point.

"Are you Harmony Carson?"

"I might be."

He looked at me with a lopsided grin. "Might be? You aren't sure whether you're Harmony Carson?"

"Who are you exactly?"

The dogs had followed me into the house, but not one of them seemed to feel threatened by the man. Even Denali, who was a wolf hybrid and didn't take kindly to strangers, trotted right over and sat at his feet as if he was a long-lost friend.

"My name's Shredder," he answered after a pause. "And this," he glanced at the Border collie, "is Riptide."

"Shredder? Who names their kid Shredder?" I didn't wait for an answer. "Never mind. What I really want to know is what you're doing in my living room."

He pulled a photo out of his pocket and handed it to me. "I understand you've been looking for this man."

"I have," I confirmed as I recognized the man from the photo Tim had sent to Harley. "Do you know him?"

"I do. Why have you been looking for him?"

I narrowed my gaze. I didn't know this man from Adam and wasn't sure I should tell him anything. "Why do you want to know?" I countered.

"It's classified."

I rolled my eyes. Oh please. Was this displaced beach boy actually trying to convince me he was some sort of a government agent? "Look, I don't know who you are or why you're here, and I certainly don't know why a grown man would pretend to be some sort of spy, but I do know you've broken into my house and I think you should leave." I reached my hand toward the rifle leaning against the wall, picked it up, and put it up against my shoulder to prove the seriousness of my statement.

Shredder chuckled. "I see you're prepared."

"I live in Alaska. You never know when you'll need to defend yourself from a predator. Human or otherwise."

"Have you ever killed anything with that gun?"

"That's none of your business. I don't know why you think it's okay to break into someone's house and make yourself comfortable without the benefit of an invitation, but it's been a long day and I have dinner to tend to, so this conversation is over."

"Actually, we've only just begun."

I pointed the gun at him. "I think we're finished."

He stood up but otherwise held his ground. "We may have gotten off on the wrong foot."

"You think?"

"I agree I probably should have waited until you got home instead of letting myself in, but I'm not used to the bracing cold you all enjoy, so I decided to wait inside. The man in the photo is someone I've been looking for, for a very long time. He's a slippery one and the trail had gone cold until I was alerted that someone had run a facial recognition program against a photo of the weasel. When I realized that photo had been taken recently, I tracked the trace to a man named Landon Stanford. He explained to me that you're looking for the man on behalf of a friend. It's imperative I find this man, so I need you to tell me everything you know."

"Tell you everything I know? Are you nuts? I don't know you and you certainly don't look like a fed. Are you some sort of bounty hunter?"

"I'm not a bounty hunter, and who I work for isn't important. What *is* important is that the man in the photo is very dangerous. If he isn't found, innocent people will die."

I dropped the angle of the gun just a bit so it was pointing at the floor and not this Shredder's chest. "'Innocent people will die'? Don't you think you're being just a bit melodramatic?"

"You believe the man is responsible for the death of your friend."

"Well, yeah."

"I'm simply saying there are others who'll die as well if he isn't found and detained."

I supposed the gorgeous beach boy had a point. "You need my help in locating this man."

"I do."

"And finding him is important to you."

"It is."

"Then it seems to me that I hold all the cards, so I'm asking you again, who are you and who do you work for?"

Shredder groaned.

I stood my ground and didn't say another word.

"Do you have a phone?" he asked.

"Of course I have a phone."

Shredder held out his hand. I handed it to him and he dialed. Then he handed it back to me.

"This is the information line for the Central Intelligence Agency. How can I help you?" a female voice said on the other end.

I glanced at Shredder. He held out his hand and I handed him the phone.

"Hey, love, it's Shredder. Can you please vouch for me?"

Shredder handed the phone back to me. I listened as the woman instructed me to cooperate with Shredder in any way he required.

I hung up and looked at him again. "You dialed the phone. How do I know that was really the CIA? It could have been your sister or your girlfriend pretending to be the CIA. Now, if you'll kindly leave so I can get on with my evening, that would be greatly appreciated."

Shredder chucked. "You're a tough one. Google the number for general information for the CIA and compare it to the number I called."

I looked at him with suspicion but did as he suggested. The numbers matched. If this was a scam, he was good at what he did. I was trying to make up my mind what to do next when I glanced at Denali. I wasn't sure if I could trust Shredder, but Denali seemed to, and he was generally a good judge of character. The silly dog, who tended to be protective and aggressive, was leaning against Shredder like he was some sort of long-lost relative. I frowned as I noticed the empty spot on the sofa. "Did you see where Honey went?"

"Honey?"

"The dog who was sitting with you when I got here. She's due to deliver any minute and I want to be sure she's okay." I headed down the hallway without giving the strange man in my living room another thought. "Honey," I called as I entered my bedroom. I didn't see her, but I heard whining coming from the closet. The door had only been open a crack, but I opened it a little farther so I could get a look at what was happening inside. "Are you okay, sweetie?" I knelt down and placed my hand on Honey's stomach.

She let out a yelp as I worked my way down toward the birth canal.

"Is she okay?" Shredder said from behind me. I was startled to find him standing there and realized I'd tossed the gun on the unmade bed, right next to a pile of clean laundry, when I'd heard Honey's whine.

"I think she's having her pups. I just found her a week ago, malnourished and weak. She's grown stronger, but I still suspect she'll need help with the delivery."

"What can I do?"

I took a deep breath and blew it out in an effort to calm my nerves. "I want to stay with her. Take the other dogs out of the room, then boil some water and get some rags out of the closet at the end of the hallway. I'll need scissors, forceps, and antiseptic. I already sterilized the items I'd need; they're in plastic bags in the bathroom. Oh, and grab my cell in case I need to call the veterinarian."

Honey let out another yelp as soon as Shredder left the room. Then she started to pant, so I began to pant along with her. I wasn't sure it was necessary, but I'd seen birth coaches panting with mothers on television and decided to give it a try.

"It's okay," I encouraged. "Everything's going to be fine. I know it hurts right now, but I'm here with you and we'll get through this. In a couple of hours, you'll have four adorable puppies."

Honey lay her head on the soft blanket I'd placed under it, but she continued to keep her eyes on me, so I kept talking in a soothing tone of voice. "Have you picked out names?" I asked as I ran my hand softly over her belly. "I guess we don't know how many boys and girls you're going to have. I should have asked Kelly. She's the one who did the ultrasound. I bet she knows."

"Here's the stuff you asked for," Shredder said as he knelt beside me. "I'm not a dog doctor, but should she be panting that heavily?"

"I don't know," I admitted. "I've rescued a lot of dogs, but I've never assisted at any births. Sit with her. I'm going to call the vet."

Shredder took over the role of calming Honey while I spoke to Justine. Kelly was out on a large animal call, but Justine assured me that most dogs managed to deliver their pups on their own. She asked me to check a few things, which I did.

"How long has she been in labor?" Justine asked.

"I don't know. She just went into the closet about twenty minutes ago, but she already seems exhausted."

"Okay, you might want to check her to see if there's a pup in the birth canal."

I glanced at Shredder, who must have noticed my slightly pale complexion because he took the phone from me and asked what to do. I held Honey's head while Shredder followed Justine's instructions. Before I even knew what was happening, a blond Lab puppy slid into his hands. Shredder grabbed one of the towels I'd sterilized and lay the pup on it. He removed the sack from its body and cut the cord, then wrapped the pup in the towel and told me to gently rub it dry while he went in for pup number two. By the time Kelly arrived an hour later, Honey was resting comfortably with her four tiny, but seemingly healthy, puppies.

"You did good." Kelly hugged me.

I glanced at Shredder. "I had help. Are they going to be okay?"

"I hope so. They're small, so I'll need you to supplement the milk they get from Honey with the formula I gave you when you first came in. I'll come back tomorrow to check on them."

"Okay." I smiled. "Thanks."

After Kelly finished her exam, I walked her out, then returned to the living room, where Shredder was waiting.

"Thank you," I said to the man who looked as exhausted as I felt.

Shredder shrugged.

"I'm kind of hungry. I was going to heat up some soup. Would you like some?"

"Sure, I could eat," Shredder answered. "You have yourself quite the houseful."

"At this point, Rescue doesn't have an animal shelter. I do what I can, but someone just donated a warehouse for us to convert into one, so by this time next year, we'll have a place to take the strays that end up on the streets."

"Something tells me you'll still have a full house." Shredder made grilled cheese sandwiches while I heated a couple of cans of cream of tomato soup.

I laughed. "Yeah, probably. I'm a sucker for anything on four legs."

When the food was ready, Shredder and I sat down at my small kitchen table while all the dogs, including Riptide, chowed down on their own meal. My dogs were used to having strange dogs come and go, so they weren't bothered by our canine visitor, and apparently, Riptide had been well socialized as well.

"So, are you going to tell me what you know about the man in the photo?" Shredder asked.

"First, why don't you tell me who he is?"

"He goes by many aliases, but his most recent seems to be Pickard."

"That's it? Just Pickard?"

"That's it."

"And why exactly have you been tracking him?"

"He deals in black market information, which basically means he steals information from one source and sells it to another."

"What kind of information?"

"All kinds. He's probably the world's best hacker. Given enough time, he can probably get into any system regardless of the security. He doesn't seem to have an allegiance to any person or country. He appears to be in it strictly for the money. If you want information and can pay for it, he can get it for you."

I cringed at the possibilities.

"The man's a ghost," Shredder continued. "We have eyes on practically every border, airport, and shipping yard in the world, but we've never been able to spot him. He somehow manages to get into the most secure databases in the world, get the information he wants, and then get out without leaving a trail. The photo your friend's been circulating is the first real lead we've had in a very long time. I need to know where you got it and why you're looking for him."

I decided any man who would stick around to help deliver puppies was most likely trustworthy, so I decided to share part of what I knew. "It all started when Tim Maverick sent a letter to Harley Medford."

"Harley Medford the actor?"

I nodded. "He grew up here and was friends with Tim when they were younger. They stayed in touch. Anyway, Tim sent Harley a photo of your information dealer and a short note saying that if he died suddenly, the man in the photo was the one responsible. When Tim died of a heroin overdose a couple of weeks later, Harley came to Rescue to look in to it. He asked me to help him and I agreed."

"And where's Harley now?"

"In Italy. There was a miscommunication with his agent, who signed Harley up to do a small part in an independent film. Harley had planned to be in Rescue through the first of the year, but he had to follow through on the commitment his agent made on his behalf, so he left last week. He said he'd worked it out to be back before Christmas."

"Okay. So, what have you discovered so far?"

"Harley and I asked around, and most everyone who knew Tim agreed he'd been clean in the days leading up to his death. We searched his cabin and didn't find any drug paraphernalia. It's our theory that the man in the photo knew Tim had a prior drug habit and used that fact to fake an accidental overdose. We believe the man was somehow linked to a job Tim had recently taken as a courier, and that something went wrong and he killed Tim. Harley and I began searching for the man, which is where you came in. Do you think Tim was somehow involved in the theft of sensitive information?"

"Maybe. You said he was working as a courier. My guess is he was pegged to serve as the middle man. He probably picked up the information that was to be sold and delivered it to the buyer. If I know Pickard, Tim did all the legwork, while he remained safely hidden."

"If this guy is stealing information, why would he need a courier? Why not just email it to his customer?"

"Pickard is too smart to leave a trail. My guess is, he downloads the information directly to a thumb drive, which is delivered to the customer. It's probably encrypted. Once Pickard gets his cash, he most likely sends the decryption key to the customer."

I frowned. "It still seems like there should be a trail of some sort to follow."

"Trust me, the best minds in the world have tried."

"So, now that you suspect this Pickard is in Alaska, how do you plan to find him? It appears Tim didn't tell anyone where he went on his delivery jobs."

"We'll need to smoke him out."

"How?"

"You said Tim's place had been tossed?"

"It was completely destroyed. Everything was pulled from the cupboards and closets, the sofa cushions had been slit, and everything that was breakable was shattered. I remember thinking whoever trashed the place must have been looking for something small."

"Like a thumb drive."

I nodded. "Exactly like a thumb drive."

"The fact that Tim's place was trashed indicates to me that the transaction he was involved in was never completed. We need to find out what your friend picked up, where he picked it up, and what he did with it once he had it. I'll be back in the morning and we'll begin our investigation."

Shredder got up and pulled on his heavy coat. He called Riptide to his side, turned, and looked at me one last time, then wandered out into the night. He hadn't even given me the opportunity to agree, which I was pretty sure wasn't a request.

Chapter 8

Saturday, December 16

Shredder was sitting at my kitchen table nursing a cup of coffee and Riptide was sleeping by the fire when I returned from walking the dogs the next day. Honey hadn't been up to going with us, so I'd taken her out for a quick bathroom break and then fed her the supplements. All in all, feeding the puppies and seeing to Honey's needs had taken up a good part of the morning, so the other dogs and I had gotten a late start.

"I see you made yourself right at home." I pulled off my gloves and hat and hung them on a peg near the door.

"It's almost ten o'clock."

"Thanks for the information, but I've been able to tell time for quite a few years now. What do you want?" I slid off my snow boots and left them to dry on the rack I'd installed for just that purpose.

"I told you I'd be by." Shredder bent down to scratch Denali behind the ears.

"You did," I acknowledged as I padded across the room in my sock-covered feet. "But I didn't say I'd be available."

"I guess you have a point." Shredder smiled, a cooked sort of smile that made him look both innocent and approachable. "Harmony Carson, do you think you can find time in your busy day to help me track down the man who most likely killed your friend Tim and will most likely be responsible for the deaths of many others if we don't stop him?"

I poured myself a cup of coffee. "Do you think he's still in the area?"

"I don't know. To be honest, I'm not sure he was ever in Rescue. At the very least I'm hoping to pick up his trail."

I took a sip of my coffee, then sat down at the table across from Shredder. "And how is it exactly that you think I can help you?"

"Prior to my arrival, you were in the process of following Tim Maverick's last days, attempting to find out how he really died. If he was supposed to deliver a package for Pickard but failed to do so—which is the assumption I'm working from at the moment—I think resolving the specifics concerning his death is still the best course of action to track Pickard. Pickard hasn't been an easy man to find and I don't have any knowledge of Tim's personal habits or the basic geography of this area. That's where you come in."

I took another sip of my coffee. I needed a minute to think about that. Getting involved in some sort of

CIA operation wasn't at all how I'd envisioned spending my day.

"Will you help me?" Shredder asked again.

"I already have a lot on my plate. I have the new pups, my other animals to care for, a shelter to remodel, the holiday to prepare for, and my job, to name just a few of my obligations."

"You were trying to find Tim's killer anyway," Shredder said.

He had a point.

"We seem to have the same agenda. All I'm asking is that we work on it as a team."

"What exactly does that mean?" I asked. "A team? Are you going to share with me what you already know?"

"I'll share what I can," Shredder answered.

"And our search for Tim's killer won't interrupt my ability to care for my animals or help out with any rescues that might come up?"

"I can agree to that."

"And my job?"

"I'll speak to your boss about a leave of absence."

"I have bills to pay, you know."

"I believe I can arrange to pay you as a consultant. Do we have a deal?"

Against my better judgment, I felt myself nodding. "Yeah. We have a deal."

"Great." Shredder grinned. "So, about breakfast…"

"I have to feed Honey and the pups before I do anything else, but you can help yourself to whatever you can find."

Shredder headed to the refrigerator, where I kept the puppy formula. "How about I help you with the feeding and then I'll take you out for a bite? We can come up with a strategy while we eat."

I wanted to say no, but I nodded instead. Shredder took out the formula and followed me to my bedroom. We poured the formula into the bottles Kelly had left and I handed two of them to Shredder.

"They look bigger already," he commented as he cradled a chocolate-colored Lab mix in his large, tan hand.

"I know it doesn't make sense that they would have already grown, but they really do look bigger," I agreed as I fed a golden-colored pup. "Of course, they've been eating nonstop since they were born."

"Honey looks like she's doing well," Shredder added.

"Yeah, I think she's going to be fine. She's been sleeping a lot, but she ate well this morning and even demonstrated a bit of energy when I took her out."

"Are you planning to keep her, or will you look for a home for her after the pups are weaned?" Shredder gently placed the pup he'd been feeding next to his siblings and picked up the next one.

"I'll probably keep Honey because I feel like we've already bonded, but I'd like to find homes for the pups. I have a few families in mind who've expressed interest in adopting a younger dog if I should come across one."

"Puppies are a lot of work," Shredder commented.

I set my first pup back in the birthing box I'd transferred the family to and picked up the last of the four waiting for her meal. "Yeah, they are. I'll need to be sure to find the right fit. I'm always very careful who I adopt the dogs and cats I find out to. I don't want any of my strays to end up back on the street."

Once all the pups had eaten, I fed Honey the second of the four small meals she was to eat each day, then took her out. And I called Kelly to tell her I'd be out but I'd leave my door unlocked in case she wanted to stop by while she was out to check on our new mom and pups. We'd decided to leave Riptide with my dogs, so as soon as I'd settled Honey back with her pups, I grabbed my backpack, jacket, hat, and gloves and followed Shredder out into the frigid morning.

There was a black Humvee parked behind my old Jeep. Shredder offered to drive, so I climbed into the passenger seat and buckled up. I assumed if he was in the CIA he'd been trained to drive in a variety of weather conditions, including snow, though based on the darkness of his tan, I was less than confident.

"So, where are you from?" I asked in what I hoped was a conversational tone.

"Nowhere in particular."

"It looks like you've spent some time in a tropical location. Unless you're into tanning booths."

Shredder glanced at me out of the corner of his eye. "No, I'm not a fan of tanning booths."

"So your last assignment was somewhere warm?"

"It would seem. Do you have a preference as to where we have breakfast?"

I knew I should suggest Chloe's Café, but she'd never allow us to talk in peace and quiet without lingering or even butting in, so I directed him to a small hunter's diner out on the highway. The likelihood of my running into anyone I knew there was a lot less than it would be in town.

I realized Shredder wasn't going to tell me where he'd gotten his tan, so I changed my line of questioning. "How long have you been with the CIA?"

"Who said I was with the CIA?"

"You did. Remember, you called them and had them vouch for you?"

"I never said I was part of the CIA, I just said they could vouch for me."

"Okay, then, who do you work for?"

"It's classified."

"Of course it is." I wasn't certain, but it seemed Shredder was enjoying our cat-and-mouse exchange. Personally, I could do with a more direct route to finding out who I was speeding down an icy highway with. "Look," I eventually said, "I've agreed to put my life on hold to team up with a stranger to find an international fugitive I know nothing about. I think it only fair that you tell me something more than your first name, which is probably an alias anyway."

"Okay. That's fair," Shredder agreed. "What do you want to know?"

"Do you work for the CIA?"

"I don't currently work for them."

"But you did at one time?"

"Sort of. I was educated by the CIA, but when it became apparent my skill set was somewhat unique, my commitment to them was forgiven so I could pursue other interests."

"Such as?"

"I'm sorry, but I really can't say."

I couldn't help but roll my eyes. This conversation was getting ridiculous. "Okay, I'll let you keep your little secret if you tell me about your family, where you grew up, and where you got that tan."

"My parents were hippies who lived in a California commune in the sixties. They lived in a group home with their free-loving friends until my mom became pregnant with me in the early eighties. At that point, they moved into a single-family home on the same piece of property. My childhood was interesting, to say the least, but that's a story for another day. As for my tan, I spent the past six months on a tropical island—and no, I can't tell you which one—and until I came to Alaska I'd never been so cold in my life."

"How did the child of a hippie couple living in a commune end up in the CIA?"

"As I've already said, I'm not a member of the CIA."

"Okay, then tell me about your education with the CIA."

"I was homeschooled until I was fourteen, by which time my dad realized I had a skill set others would find of value. He arranged for a friend of his to have me tested for a program that was run by the CIA to train young operatives."

"Are you making this up?"

Shredder turned his head and glanced at me. "Does it sound like it's made up?"

"Totally."

"I find it's best to trust your intuition."

"You realize your story makes no sense, right? Why would a hippie who lived in a commune for most of his life even consider handing his son over to a government agency?"

"There are things about me you can't know and would never understand."

"You see, it's the whole vague thing that's rubbing me wrong. It feels artificial. I feel like everything you've said to me since we met has been a lie. How do I know I can trust you?"

Shredder shrugged. "I guess you'll have to get to know me better and decide for yourself if I'm trustworthy. Is the diner on the right or the left?

"Left. In about a mile. There's a big neon sign with a moose on it. You can't miss it."

******

Luckily, the diner wasn't crowded and we settled into a booth in the back and ordered coffee and the breakfast special. The place might be a bit of a dive, but I'd eaten there before and knew they had pretty good food. It was nice and warm, so I slid out of my outerwear before taking the first sip of the strong coffee it was known for.

"Okay, what exactly is your plan?" I asked after we'd ordered and the waitress had left to help another customer.

"When I spoke to Landon, he told me that you'd already started to map Tim Maverick's last days. We'll start there."

I sat back in the booth and considered the man across from me. I still wasn't 100 percent sure I could trust him, but I'd agreed to work with him, so I needed to tell him something. The conversation paused while the waitress brought our bacon, eggs, biscuits, and gravy. We both took a few bites before I picked it up again.

"Look, I really did tell you everything I know last night. I know Tim sent the photo of Pickard to Harley and said if he died, the man in the photo had killed him. Harley and I have been asking around, and we learned Tim was a courier, most likely working for Pickard. We know Tim died of a drug overdose, even though everyone who knew him swears he was clean, and we saw for ourselves his home was tossed."

Shredder took a bite of his biscuit before he answered. "Think of the people you've spoken to in the past week. Someone must have told you something you haven't already told me."

"Tim stopped at the gas station to fill up his tank on the day before his body was found. He told Gill Greenland, the station owner, he was heading north."

"Okay, that could be a clue. What about after that?"

"So far, no one I've spoken to has said they've seen him after that."

"His body was found in Rescue?" Shredder asked.

"Just outside of town."

"So, if he took a trip north, it appears he returned home before he was murdered, if that's what happened."

"It would seem. I can't say for sure he actually went home, though."

Shredder took a sip of his coffee, his eyes on me all the while. "You said Tim's place was tossed. Do you know if that happened before or after his body was found?"

I shook my head. "I don't know when it happened. It could have been at any point before Harley, Jake, and I checked it out, which was on Thursday of last week."

"Okay, let's head over there when we're done eating. Maybe there's a clue the three of you missed."

****

Tim's cabin didn't look like it had been touched since we'd been there more than a week before. As far as I knew, Tim's death was still considered an accidental overdose, so the police hadn't initiated an investigation. Tim's parents had left Rescue quite a while ago, and had cut all ties with him when his drug habit was at its worst. I wasn't certain if they'd ever mended their relationship. If not, I had no idea who Tim might have listed as his next of kin.

"What are we looking for?" I asked.

"Anything that might point us to Tim's whereabouts during the last weeks of his life. We know he'd made contact with Pickard prior to sending the photo to Harley Medford, and at that point he considered him a threat. We don't know how long they were acquainted or where and how they met."

"Do you think that matters?"

"It might. Why don't you take a look around in here and I'll start off in the bedroom?"

I did as Shredder asked and began picking up, then discarding, items I'd found on the floor. I now assumed whoever had trashed the place was most likely looking for the thumb drive with sensitive information, if any of that story was true, but I thought it couldn't still be in the cabin, if it ever had been there at all. Of course, he might have hidden it somewhere he knew this Pickard wouldn't find it, but I didn't know Tim well enough to know where that would be.

I found a matchbook on the floor from a bar I knew was about sixty miles north of Rescue. Not a good sign because Tim was supposed to be on the wagon, but I suppose he might have simply stopped by to eat or use the facilities. Tim had been heading north the day before his body was found, so I set it aside. I also found a receipt for gas dated the same day. Gill had said Tim stopped by for gas on his way north, so if the receipt was in the cabin, it suggested Tim had completed his trip and come home before being assaulted by the man who killed him, assuming, of course, his drug overdose really was the result of someone shooting him up against his will. If he'd completed his trip, did that mean he'd handed the thumb drive off to the person he was supposed to deliver it to?

Toward the bottom of a pile of books on the floor, I found a small notepad, the sort you might keep next to your phone. The pages were all blank, but I could see indentations on the first one from whatever had been written on the previous page. I looked around until I found a pencil, then scratched it over the surface. The paper said *Grizzly Inn 6 pm*. There wasn't a date, so I had no way of knowing if the note related to something that had happened immediately before Tim's death, but I knew the place was about three hours north of town.

"Did you find anything?" Shredder asked when I came out to the main room.

"A gas receipt, a matchbook, and a note."

"Sounds promising. What do they tell you?"

I held up the receipt first. "When I spoke to Gill, he told me Tim had filled up his vehicle the day before his body was found and was heading north. This receipt is from that day. To me, that means he most likely completed whatever task he'd had for the day and came home before he died."

"Is it possible Tim went to buy the gas, came home and dropped off the receipt, and then headed north?"

"Possible, sure. Likely, no."

"Did anyone you spoke to know for sure that Tim's trip north had to do with his courier job?"

"No. No one other than Gill told me he was even heading north. There are too many unanswered questions at this point to begin to develop a viable theory as to exactly what Tim was doing."

Shredder frowned. "Okay, so let's go with the assumption Tim went north the day before his death to drop off whatever it was he was supposed to deliver."

"It would seem so."

Shredder picked up a phone book, then tossed it aside. "What else did you find?"

I held up the matchbook. "This is from a bar about sixty miles north of here. I have no way of knowing when Tim picked it up, but I also found this notepad. The last note Tim made dealt with the Grizzly Inn, which is about three hours north. It's possible Tim stopped off at the bar on his way back from meeting someone at the inn."

"Is there anything else on the note?"

"Just a time: Six pm. I guess we could call the inn to see if anyone who works there knows whether Tim met someone there the day before he died."

Shredder shook his head. "It'd be better to drive up there and talk to the desk clerk in person. I found something in the bedroom that leads me to believe Tim may have visited that inn on other occasions."

Shredder handed me Tim's credit card statement. There were three charges for the Grizzly Inn in the past two months. All appeared to be one-night stays. One charge was for the night he died.

"I think we should go up there," Shredder repeated. "Maybe spend the night."

"What about the puppies? They need to be bottle-fed four times a day."

"Is there anyone you can hire to stay at your house?"

Today was Saturday, which meant the veterinary office would be closed the next day. Justine had helped me out with my animals before when I'd been out of town. As long as we were back by dinnertime, she might be willing to spend the night at my house. "I do have someone I can ask, but we'd need to be back before dinner tomorrow at the latest."

"Call your friend. If you can get someone to take care of the animals, I'll call to reserve two rooms at the inn for tonight."

"Do you want to leave Riptide with the other dogs?"

Shredder hesitated.

"I'm not sure the inn allows pets."

"Okay. He seems to like hanging out at your place and I guess it would be easier."

"Do you take him with you everywhere you go?"

"If I can."

Justine was happy to help, so I had Shredder drop me at my house, where I hurriedly cleaned up a bit, fed all the animals, including the puppies, and exercised the dogs. Then I tossed a few things in an overnight bag before calling Jake to let him know I'd be out of town until the following evening. Jake was, of course, curious where I was going, with whom, and why. I filled him in the best I could without giving too much away over the phone, which I knew was far from secure. Shredder pulled up minutes after I finally convinced Jake I'd be fine and not to worry. Justine would be over when she got off work, so I left the front door unlocked and instructions for all the animals on the kitchen counter.

I glanced at the dark sky as we pulled onto the highway. "It looks like we're in for some more snow."

"Does it snow every day here?"

"Not every day, but it snows a lot. I assume you packed emergency supplies? It isn't safe to travel this road without food, water, blankets, flares, flashlights, a fire starter, and a first aid kit."

"I have everything we need should we become stranded. Did your friend show up?"

"She'll be by after work. Did you fill up the tank? It's a ways until the next gas station."

"I topped it off on my way to pick you up. Have you told anyone where we're going or what we hope to find?" he asked.

"Justine just knows I had to go out of town. She didn't ask any questions and I didn't offer any information. Jake asked lots of questions when I called him. You spoke to him about my having time off, right? He must have believed whatever story you told him because he agreed to it, but he's always concerned about me. He wanted to know exactly where I was going, but I just told him we had a lead to follow up and I'd be out of town until tomorrow. I agreed to check in with him later tonight so he knows we reached our destination in one piece. He wasn't happy I wouldn't tell him more, but he knew there wasn't anything he could do to stop me from doing what I believed I needed to do."

"Do you think Jake has told anyone else we're working together?"

"Not if you asked him not to."

"When I spoke to him, I made sure he understood how important it was to be discreet."

"Then you can trust him to keep what he knows to himself."

Snow had begun to fall and Shredder turned the windshield wipers on low. "When I spoke to Jake about giving you time off to help me with my project, I got the impression you two had more than an employer/employee relationship. Are you dating?"

"Jake's my brother-in-law."

"I see. I didn't realize you had a sister."

"I don't anymore. She died during a rescue when I was seventeen."

"I'm sorry."

I let out a long breath. "Yeah, me too. Do you have any siblings?"

"No, I'm an only child. I don't think my parents would even have had me if nature hadn't intervened. To be honest, I always felt like an intruder in their lives."

"You were their son. I doubt they saw you that way."

Shredder paused before answering. "My parents were really in to each other and the commune. Having a child put limitations on their activities. My dad told me that he knew my IQ was exceptional and I'd be an asset to my country, which was why they were willing to give me up, but I could tell he was glad I was going."

I put my hand to my chest. "That's so sad."

Shredder shrugged. "It worked out okay. I love my life and my work, and I do feel my presence on this earth makes a difference."

"Do you still see your parents?"

"I haven't seen them since the day I left the commune."

I was pretty sure I was going to cry. Shredder had parents he never saw by choice, while I'd give quite a lot to see my parents even one more time. It did sound like his parents had abandoned him, so I supposed I could understand how he felt.

"I hacked into Tim's credit card account when I got back to the place I've been staying to get my things. The last charge was for the Grizzly Inn the night he left Rescue to head north."

"So that must have been where he was going. I wonder what happened between the time he checked out of the inn and when his body was found."

"I'm sure the answer to that question will reveal quite a lot. It would be easier if someone had seen him during those critical hours."

"Just because no one I've spoken to has doesn't mean no one did. I guess we just keep asking."

Shredder didn't respond, so I leaned forward to turn on the radio. Before I could find a station I liked, an image flashed in my mind. I closed my eyes and focused. "Someone's in trouble."

Chapter 9

"What do you mean?" Shredder asked as he slowed the vehicle and turned to look at me.

I kept my eyes closed so I wouldn't lose the connection. "I can see people I'm meant to help in some way."

"See them?"

"I'll explain later. I see a car. It's slid into a ditch. There are four people inside, two adults and two children."

I could feel Shredder slowing the vehicle even more before he eventually pulled over to the side and stopped.

"Are they on this road?" Shredder asked.

I took a deep breath and focused my energy. The driver, a man, was injured. He'd hit his head when the car slid into the ditch. I sensed he was clinging to life. The woman in the front seat was unconscious, but not seriously injured. There was a little girl of around five or six in a booster seat in the back, along with a toddler in a car seat. Both of the kids were screaming hysterically.

I knew I needed to find them, and fast. I put my head in my hands and began to rub my forehead, still without opening my eyes. "They're on a road that turns off from this one. A private road, I think. I can see a structure in the background. A house, I think, but I'm not sure. It's dark."

I took several deep breaths and focused harder. "Drive forward slowly. Look for a road that veers off to the left. It isn't well-traveled and won't be easy to spot."

I could feel the vehicle begin to pull forward. I focused all my energy on the girl in the backseat. She stopped crying and looked around. *"We're coming for you,"* I said with my mind.

"Where are you?" the girl said aloud.

"I need you to crawl into the front seat and turn on the headlights so we can see you," I instructed.

"But there's too much blood. I think my dad is dead. My mom too."

"They aren't dead," I assured her.

"I still don't see anything," Shredder said.

I held up my hand but didn't answer. I couldn't afford to break the link I had with the child.

"I can't do it," the girl cried. "I'm too scared. Why can't I see you?"

"I'm coming for you. I'll be there soon, but I need you to do it."

I could feel the girl's terror as she slowly climbed over the seat. She sobbed loudly as she looked for the headlight switch.

"On the left," I instructed. *"That little knob near your dad's hand."*

I could see the girl pull the knob. The area around the car was illuminated by the headlights. I was surprised the couple had been driving with the lights off in the first place. Based on what I could see, the accident hadn't occurred much before I'd first picked up the connection.

"I see a light. Off to the left," Shredder said.

"Head toward it. There'll be a road. You'll have to look carefully," I said.

Shredder pulled onto the road, then stopped. We both jumped out and headed toward the car, which had settled on its side. I wedged the back door open and the girl I'd connected with flew into my arms. Shredder unbuckled the screaming toddler while I took the girl in my arms back to Shredder's Humvee. Once both children were settled onto the backseat, we returned for the adults.

"We need an ambulance," Shredder said as he felt for a pulse after pulling the man from the vehicle and settling him onto the snow. "He's alive, but just barely."

I held up my phone, but I had no lines.

"I have a satellite phone in the glove box," Shredder informed me. He looked up at the falling snow. "I'm not sure it'll work with the snow."

"I'll check." I got up and ran to the Humvee while Shredder worked on extracting the woman from the car.

"Are they going to be okay?" the girl cried as I slid into the front passenger seat to look for Shredder's phone.

"I hope so." I took out the satellite phone, but it also was devoid of a signal. "We need to get them to a hospital, but the phones aren't working."

"The house," the girl informed me. "There's a radio in the house."

Of course: the house I'd seen in my vision.

"It's just down the road," the girl added.

"Okay. Wait here. I'm going to help carry your parents to the Humvee."

Shredder picked up the woman and headed toward the vehicle.

"What happened?" the woman asked as she regained consciousness.

"You were in an accident," Shredder answered as he carried her to the vehicle.

"Hope and Faith?" The woman began to struggle.

"They're fine," I said.

Shredder set the woman down and she climbed in with her daughters while we returned for the man. He still hadn't regained consciousness, so we lay him in the cargo area of the Humvee, then Shredder drove toward the house. The woman knew who to call for help, so we left her to it while we settled the injured man onto the bed.

"Help is on the way."

The woman put her hand to her mouth. "Is he alive?"

"Yes," Shredder confirmed. "I've had some medical training, but I'm not a doctor. The sooner help arrives the better. Do you have medical supplies?"

The woman nodded and left the room.

"Hold this towel over the cut on his head," Shredder instructed. "We need to stop the bleeding."

I did as Shredder instructed. He began to remove the man's clothing, carefully looking for additional injuries as he did. The woman returned with a medical kit. Shredder thanked her, then suggested she go see to her children.

"Will he live?" I asked.

"I don't know. He's lost a lot of blood."

"What can I do?"

"Pray."

I tried to calm my jangled nerves as I did just that. I really needed Moose right then, but he obviously wasn't within reach, so I needed to refocus my energy on my own. At least the girl I'd connected with hadn't been injured. I could feel her terror, but I'm not sure how I would have dealt with her pain as well.

"Are you okay?" Shredder asked.

I nodded. "Making a psychic connection takes a lot out of me. I need a few minutes to recover."

"I can handle this myself."

I shook my head. "No. I want to help." I glanced at the man's bare torso. "It looks like he has a broken rib."

Shredder frowned. "Yeah. It looks pretty bad. We need to be careful not to move him any more than we have. I hope I didn't puncture his lung when I pulled him out of the car."

"You had to get him out. He would have bled to death."

"I know. It was the only choice. How's the head doing?"

I lifted the towel. The blood flow had slowed. I wasn't sure if that was a good thing or a bad one.

I could see headlights out the window as a car pulled up. A man carrying a dark bag got out. I could hear the woman greet him and then lead him toward the room.

"This is Doc Barnes. He lives down the road a bit."

I was hoping for an ambulance but was relieved to turn the responsibility for the man's life over to a doctor, who set his bag on a nearby table and began to discuss the injuries with Shredder. I could see the men had it under control, so I followed the woman into the living room, where the children were watching a DVD.

"I'm so grateful you found us," the woman said, tears spilling from her eyes. "When the accident first happened, I was sure no one would see us before we all froze to death. We were far enough off the main road that a car passing by wouldn't see us, and Kurt must have hit the headlight switch when we rolled because everything went dark. I tried to get out of my seat belt, but I guess I must have passed out because the next thing I knew, your friend was carrying me to his vehicle."

I was going to explain that we would never have found them if her older daughter hadn't been brave enough to accept my voice in her head and follow my instructions, but the woman had been through enough. I made a comment about God's intervention and left it at that. I sat down on the sofa and the older girl, who was Faith, crawled into my lap. She put her arms around me and hugged me tight.

"Thank you for coming," she whispered into my ear.

"Thank you for allowing me to talk to you and then following my instructions."

"When I heard your voice but couldn't see you, I thought you must be an angel. Are you an angel?"

I pulled the warm child closer to my body. "No. Not an angel. But I do have a gift that allows me to talk to people who are in need of saving. Most of the people I talk to aren't as brave as you, though. Most try to block me out. You're a very special girl."

"That's what Mama always says."

I felt the girl's tears through my shirt. She'd been so brave, but I knew an experience like this could take a lot out of you. I felt my own heart rate slow to normal as we waited to find out her father's fate. It seemed I didn't need Moose after all; the child in my arms helped me to harness my emotions and focus my energy.

She fell asleep after a while, but I continued to hold her and accept comfort from her warmth. I was about to doze off myself when the sound of sirens in the distance penetrated my mind. Once the ambulance arrived, everything happened quickly. Both the man and woman were transported to the hospital. A neighbor came to stay with the girls until their aunt arrived. I hated to leave them, but they seemed fine with the neighbor, and Shredder and I had other dragons to slay.

Chapter 10

The Grizzly Inn, which catered to hunters and fishermen during the summer, spring, and fall, was rustic. During the month of December, it played host to people from the area who came to the small town looking for the magic of Christmas. I'd stayed there years before, when my parents had brought Val and me for a family summer vacation. I'd always wanted to come back at Christmas, but until now I hadn't gotten around to it.

"I feel like we traveled through a wormhole and came out in North Pole City," Shredder commented as we drove slowly along the main street running through town.

"I know what you mean. I keep expecting to see Santa walking down the street." I glanced out the window at the colorfully lit shops, candy cane lampposts, and the huge tree in the town square. "It's nice, though. Oh, look." I pointed at a group of carolers dressed in Victorian garb.

"You must really be in to Christmas."

"Not really. My parents died in late December when I was thirteen and Val died almost exactly four years later. Most of the time I just want the holiday to pass. But I have to say I'm finding this town charming. I guess being able to help Faith's family has given me a bit of the Christmas spirit this year."

"So, are you going to tell me how you did that?"

I hated for Shredder to see me as a freak. After what he'd witnessed, he most likely already did, so I didn't see the harm in telling him the truth. "I have the ability to connect psychically with people I'm supposed to help. Usually, it's a one-way connection; I can see and feel them, but they can't see or feel me. Occasionally, I'm able to achieve a two-way connection, and the person can feel my presence. I've never before been able to actually converse with the person I connected with the way I did with Faith. She could hear my voice in her head and I could see what needed to be done, so I told her. It was pretty spectacular."

"That's amazing."

I shrugged. "There are times, like tonight, when I consider my ability a gift. But there are other times when all I can do is stand by and watch and feel the person I've connected to die. Then I know my gift is really a curse."

Shredder turned into the parking lot in front of the lodge. He parked and turned off the vehicle, then turned and looked at me. "Can you control it? Can you make the choice to connect or not?"

I unbuckled my seat belt. "The ability to connect seems to be somehow predetermined. A picture just pops into my head and I know I'm supposed to stop and pay attention. I've been working on making intentional connections, but it doesn't always work. A week or so ago I was at the bar and we got a call about two women lost in a storm. I hadn't felt them up to that point, but I got as much information as I could, then sat down and focused. I was able to make a one-way connection with them. I could see and sense them but not vice versa. It turned out they were okay, but the man who was with them died."

"If you connect to someone you know you can't save, can you turn it off?"

"I don't know; I've never tried. I know my ability to connect is important. If I can't save them and they're destined to die, maybe I can bring them a sense of peace in their final moments."

"You're an exceptional woman."

I blushed but didn't respond.

Shredder opened his door and stepped out into the snow. I did the same. The exterior of the inn was decorated in colorful Christmas lights and the trees near the front entry were covered with little white twinkle lights. By unspoken agreement, we headed inside to register first. We could come back for our things once we knew which rooms we were assigned to.

"It's really beautiful with all the fresh snow," I said as we walked into the log building. "I know we're here to dig up information on Tim, but it would be fun to walk around town after we check in."

"I'm fine with that," Shredder commented. "This will be the first white Christmas I've had in years."

"Do you think you'll still be in Alaska at Christmas?"

Shredder paused. "I'm not sure. But we're here tonight and the town is all decked out. I say we enjoy the festivities."

He opened the log door and motioned for me to precede him.

The lobby was cheerfully decorated with holly and red ribbons, and a huge tree was artfully decorated in the seating area near the huge, floor-to-ceiling fireplace. Christmas carols played in the background, and someone had left coffee and Christmas cookies on a table nearby.

"Check in for Mr. Jones," Shredder said.

The woman opened her reservation book and frowned. "It says here you were supposed to arrive before five. It's almost seven."

"We ran into an auto accident on the way and stopped to lend a hand. Is there a problem with checking in now?"

"Not if you don't mind sharing a room. I'm afraid we gave away one of the rooms you reserved when you didn't arrive when indicated."

Shredder looked at me.

"Are there two beds in the room?" I asked.

"Two queens," the woman replied.

I turned to Shredder and nodded.

"We'll take the one room," Shredder informed the desk clerk.

After we'd been given our keys and room number, we returned to the Humvee to get our bags. We both had blood on the clothes we were wearing under our jackets, so we wanted to wash up before heading back outside. Our room was actually very nice. The two beds were situated one on either side of a small, white brick fireplace. The carpet and curtains were white as well, and the bedspreads were a cheerful Christmas red. There was a white dresser on one wall and an adjoining bathroom with both a shower and a tub.

"Nice room," I said aloud.

"It'll do. Why don't you use the bathroom first? I need to make a couple of calls."

I grabbed my bag and placed it on one of the beds. "You don't have to offer twice. I can't wait to shower the blood off my arms." I grabbed some clothes and headed into the bathroom. I turned the water on hot, stripped off my clothes, and stepped into the hard spray. I felt myself relax as the water massaged my shoulders.

I thought about the family we'd helped as I squeezed shampoo onto my dark hair. It seemed the mother and daughters would be fine, but I wasn't as certain about the father. He'd been in pretty bad shape when they'd taken him away in the ambulance. I hoped he'd survive the ride to the hospital. The woman had given Shredder her contact information. Maybe I'd have him call her later to see how the family was doing.

As I rinsed my hair I turned my thoughts to Tim. I supposed Shredder and I should come up with some sort of a plan to obtain the information we were after. I could lie and say Tim was my brother who had disappeared and I was trying to retrace his steps, but that could be tricky. As long as we didn't come across anyone who knew what had really happened to Tim we'd be okay, but if whatever he was involved in had happened here, it would be hard to know who we could trust.

I turned off the shower, rang the water from my long hair, and wrapped a thick towel around my body. A quick inspection of my hands and arms confirmed that I'd managed to get off all the blood. I wasn't certain my clothes would be that lucky. I only had blood on the blouse I'd been wearing under my coat, but poor Shredder, who had carried the injured man from the car, had blood on his jacket and his sweater. Fortunately, he had an extra jacket in his luggage and had changed into it after the ambulance arrived. I'd asked him why he had two jackets and he'd said you never knew when you'd need to change your look to evade a tail.

Pretty much everything Shredder said convinced me he was a spy of some sort. He seemed strong and decisive, and I had no doubt he could handle any situation. I could picture him shooting someone if he had to, yet he had a gentle and tender side that kept me guessing. Who was this man I'd agreed to an overnight adventure with? Could I trust him? Or had he been lying to me since the first moment I laid eyes on him? All the uncertainty surrounding his past and even his present didn't sit well with me.

Once I'd dressed in a red flannel shirt, a warm pullover sweater, and a clean pair of jeans, I gathered my things and went out to the bedroom. Shredder was writing something in a small black book, which he slipped into his suitcase when he noticed me watching him.

"All done?" he asked.

"The bathroom's all yours."

"Great." He picked up his change of clothes and shut the lid of his suitcase.

I waited until I heard the water go on in the bathroom, then wandered over to his suitcase. I knew I shouldn't snoop, but I couldn't help it. I tried to open the bag, but it was locked. I should have known Shredder wouldn't make it that easy.

I put my soiled clothes in the plastic bag the inn supplied for laundry and began to comb out my hair. Then I pulled the inn's landline toward me and dialed my home number. Justine was there and answered the phone on the second ring. She assured me that my entire animal family were fed, exercised, and tucked in and I didn't have a thing to worry about. Justine loved animals and I knew she'd take good care of them.

After that I called Jake. He was happy to hear from me, though not quite as happy and reassuring as Justine had been.

"What do you really know about this guy?" Jake asked.

"We've already been over this. I don't know a lot about him, but he seems legit, and he wants to find Tim's killer the same as I do. We came across an accident on the road and he was really great. He knew just what to do. The father of the family we helped is probably only alive because Shredder had some medical training."

"I hadn't heard about the accident. Are you okay?"

"I'm fine." I paused, then said, "I made a two-way connection. The clearest one yet. I could sense the family was in trouble and managed to connect with their five-year-old daughter. She could hear my voice in her head. I told her what I needed her to do and she did it."

"Wow. That's really something. Your abilities seem to be evolving," Jake said. "Are you sure you're okay? That had to be intense, and you didn't have Moose with you."

"I'm fine," I assured him. "The girl I connected with wasn't injured. Just scared. I think we helped each other."

"If you could master the ability to communicate with rescue victims, do you know what that would mean?"

"I could help people who are in trouble help themselves."

Jake and I both took a moment to let the significance of that sink in.

"I guess I should go," I said. "Shredder and I are going out. I'll call you in the morning."

"Okay. Have fun, but be careful."

"Always."

I hung up, then turned to see a shirtless man dressed only in soft, faded jeans, watching me.

"Was that Jake?" Shredder asked.

"Yeah. I told him I'd check in. He worries about me. I was thinking pizza for dinner. How do you feel about pizza?"

Shredder pulled a baby blue T-shirt over his head, then adjusted it over his well-defined chest. "I like pizza."

"Great. There used to be a good pizza joint in town. We can see if it's still there."

"Sounds good. I'm starving."

The inn was situated at one end of a strip of mom-and-pop shops, so we decided to bundle up and walk. There were flurries in the air, but the harder snow had passed and the temperature hovered around the freezing mark, which was warm by Alaskan standards. The energy created by the visitors as they walked around the little town, browsing through the quaint shops and enjoying the store windows, caught me up in the Christmas spirit.

I grabbed Shredder's hand. "Oh, look. Santa really is in town."

Shredder glanced in the direction I was pointing.

"We should get a photo of you sitting on Santa's lap," Shredder said.

I laughed. "Not for a million dollars."

"Come on. You don't have to sit on his lap. I'll take a photo of you standing next to him."

I'm not sure why I agreed, but Shredder could be very persuasive. He took a photo with his phone and we went on.

The pizza pub I remembered from my trip with my family was in the same place, and we grabbed a booth near the brick pizza oven and ordered a couple of beers. I'm something of a pizza purist, liking plain cheese or pepperoni over pies with multiple toppings, but Shredder liked the works, so we ordered two smalls, figuring we could take the leftovers back to the room for a late-night snack or breakfast.

"So, about the investigation…" I began after we'd ordered. "Do you have a plan?"

"I spoke to the desk clerk while you were in the shower."

"How did you have time to do that?"

"You took a long time. Anyway, she said Tim had reserved a room there seven times over the past several months. She didn't know why he was here or who he might have met, but she did say he never showed up for his last reservation."

"But the charge for the room was on his credit card," I argued.

"Apparently, Tim wanted a specific room: number ten. The inn will only guarantee a specific room if you guarantee the room with a credit card, which is charged whether you show up or not. Tim didn't cancel twenty-four hours in advance, so his card was charged."

I could see the credit card guarantee from the inn's perspective, but that meant we had no way of knowing if Tim had ever made it to his destination the day before he died. If he didn't arrive at the inn, where had he gone?

"Why room ten?" I asked.

Shredder shrugged. "I don't know. The desk clerk said he asked for that room every time. The last was the only time he didn't show."

I bit my lip as I considered that. "We know Tim got a job as a courier. Maybe he arranged to meet the person he was picking up or dropping off merchandise to in room ten. Or…" I paused as I got a really good idea. "Maybe the room was a drop point."

"So, the person who booked the room before him each time left something for him, or the person who booked it after him picked something up he'd left behind."

"Exactly. If that's what was going on, we need to find out if the same person booked the room either before or after Tim every time he was there."

Shredder took a sip of his beer before responding. "What if the person he was dropping off or picking up from was different each time?"

"Then there wouldn't be a pattern," I realized.

"We need to get a look at that room. If the occupants are already settled in for the night by the time we return, we'll have a look tomorrow. In the meantime, we can find out who rented the room before and after Tim each time he stayed at the inn."

I picked a piece of pepperoni off a slice and plopped it into my mouth. "If Tim never checked into the inn on his last trip north, I wonder if he completed his transaction?"

Shredder nibbled on a piece of pizza as he considered my question. "We know Tim headed north on the day he was supposed to arrive at the inn, but he never arrived. Considering we found the receipt for the fuel he purchased on his way out of town in his home, I have to assume that for some reason he made the decision to head home instead of going north. Now, it's possible he met his contact elsewhere and completed the transaction before heading home. Given the fact his place was tossed, it's reasonable to assume he either picked something up and headed home without delivering it or he was supposed to drop it off but never did, and the person who was to receive it went looking for it."

I sat quietly as I tried to make sense of what was turning into something very complicated. If Tim was a courier who picked up an item, such as a thumb drive, then dropped it off elsewhere, that would require two separate trips. "We need to find out what Tim was doing on the days immediately before and after his trips to the inn," I said. "If he was picking up information Pickard had stored on a thumb drive at the inn, he would have needed to arrange for a second meeting with the customer who was to receive the information on the other end. Do you think Pickard was personally delivering the drive to Tim?"

"The intel we have indicates Pickard breaks into secure databases and downloads the information he's been contracted to provide directly onto thumb drives, heavily encrypted. The customer pays for the drive, then is given the code to decrypt the information. As far as we can tell, Pickard doesn't save the information anywhere else, like a hard drive, and never forwards it via the internet. It seems like a cumbersome process, but by doing it that way he's so far managed to avoid detection and capture. The question of whether his courier has direct access to him isn't known. Until the photo Tim sent Harley, he was a virtual ghost."

"Tim has to have met him face to face at least once because he had the photo," I pointed out.

Shredder took the photo out of his pocket and looked at it closely. "Pickard is in a windowless room that could be located almost anywhere. I've been assuming he must be or have been in Alaska because Tim was working for him, but that may not be true."

He took out his phone, dialed a number, and waited for someone to pick up. "Hi, love; it's Shredder. I need a favor."

He laughed at something the person said. "Alas, not that kind of favor. I want you to pull travel records for Tim Maverick for the past year. If he boarded a plane, train, ferry, or spaceship, I want to know about it. Check passport records as well."

Shredder hung up without saying good-bye. When it came to work, he tended to forgo pleasantries.

"I wonder what Tim did—or didn't do—that got him killed," I said.

Shredder shrugged. "He knew weeks before he died that his death was a possibility. We suspect he didn't complete his last job. He could have had a plan to get out from under Pickard that backfired. Maybe he suspected it might fail, so he sent the letter."

"That would fit." I nodded. "The letter he sent Harley indicated he'd gotten himself in a bad situation and he planned to get out of it, but if it didn't work, then the man in the photo had killed him."

"It sounds like Tim made that last reservation at the inn but never intended to keep it. It may have been just a smoke screen. The question is, if he had the thumb drive and didn't deliver it, where is it?"

"Maybe we should show Pickard's photo around town," I suggested. "If the inn was a pickup point, Pickard must have been the one to meet Tim there to drop off the information."

"Not necessarily. He could have had another courier deliver the drive. It would be my guess he rarely leaves wherever it is he's holed up."

I supposed if you were an international fugitive it would make sense to stay well-hidden, which made me wonder how Tim had managed to get the photo in the first place.

After we left the pizza parlor, Shredder and I took a walk around town. I had a photo of Tim from a party we'd both attended and Shredder had the photo of Pickard, so we decided to show them around on the off chance someone had seen them. It was a long shot for sure, but it was a festive night, with the snow flurries and the Christmas decorations, so even if we came up empty, it wouldn't be a total waste of time.

I was sorting through tree ornaments in a cozy seasonal store when Shredder's phone rang. He looked at the caller ID, then stepped outside. I picked up a pair of heavy socks with pictures of moose on them that I thought would be a fun gift for Chloe. I'd been honest when I'd told Shredder I wasn't that in to Christmas after the losses I'd suffered during the season, but I still bought little trinkets for the people in my life.

"You have news?" I asked when Shredder returned.

"I do. First, the father in the accident is going to be all right."

I let out a sigh of relief. "And…?"

"And Tim traveled to Kotzebue five times in the past three months. All the dates correspond to the days just before his reservations at the inn."

"So, you think he went to Kotzebue to pick up the thumb drives, came back to Rescue, then drove to the inn to deliver the information?"

"That would be my guess."

"So Pickard must be in Kotzebue."

"Perhaps. Kotzebue could also have been a hopping-off point for Tim to rent a boat or aircraft and continue on to Russia."

Shredder made a good point. The Bering Strait, which divided Alaska from Russia, was only fifty-five miles at its narrowest. If someone wanted to get from one country to the other under the radar, that would be the way to do it. In fact, two islands in the middle of the strait, Big Diomede in Russia and Little Diomede in Alaska, were less than two and a half miles apart from each other.

"Okay. Say Pickard is hiding out in some remote part of Russia. He must travel at times. He did, after all, kill Tim in Rescue."

"We don't know that for certain. All we're sure of is that Tim died of a heroin overdose and he had reason to believe Pickard might want him dead. Based on what I know of Pickard, even if that's true, he wouldn't have done it himself. I guess I should have considered that when I headed to Rescue in the first place."

"So, are you leaving?" I asked as we walked down the festive street that suddenly seemed all wrong for the conversation we were having.

"At some point, but not tonight. I have people checking into some things. My instructions for now are to follow through and see if we can locate the thumb drive. If Tim hid it before he died, it may still be somewhere to be found." Shredder looked at his watch. "I have some work to do. Let's head back to the inn."

Chapter 11

Sunday, December 17

Shredder was gone when I woke up the next morning. There was a cheery fire in the fireplace and a pot of coffee on the small table for two, with a note letting me know he had to look in to a few things and would be back by nine. It was currently eight, so I figured I'd pour myself a cup of coffee, then have a shower while I waited.

When we'd returned to the room the previous evening, Shredder had logged on to his computer and barely said a word from that point forward. I wasn't certain how long he'd stayed up because he was still working when I fell asleep.

The coffee in the pot was still hot, so I added a dollop of cream and sat down on one of the chairs near the fire. The room really was nice, not like an average hotel room at all. It was large and cheery and nicely decorated. I figured Justine would be up because the puppies would need to be fed, so I called her to check in before I headed for the shower.

"How's everyone going?" I asked.

"Everyone's fine. I'm enjoying spending time with your family, although I almost tripped several times trying to make my way to the bathroom in the middle of the night."

"There are a lot of bodies to watch out for," I admitted. "Are the pups eating okay?"

"All four of them are little piglets. Judging by the way they're growing, you might be able to cut back on the number of supplemental feedings in a week or so. You should talk to Kelly about it."

"I will. It would be easier on my schedule not to have to be available four times a day. Is anything else going on?"

"Harley Medford called your house phone. I told him you were out of town and to try your cell."

"That's funny. I didn't get a message."

"He might not have wanted to bother you. He said he was going to be back in Rescue by the middle of next week and would see you then."

I was disappointed I'd missed Harley's call. I'd found I'd missed him since he'd been gone, which was something I definitely didn't want to do because I knew he'd be leaving for good after the first of the year. I wasn't particularly interested in having any man in my life, but if I was looking for male companionship, it certainly wouldn't be from a high-profile movie star who traveled the world and had a different beautiful woman on his arm with each movie he made.

I finished my coffee and went into the bathroom. I was dressed and ready to get on with the day by the time Shredder got back.

"Oh good, you're up," Shredder greeted me as he pulled off his jacket. "I spoke to the desk clerk, who said we could get a look at room ten at ten o'clock. In the meantime, there's a breakfast buffet downstairs if you're hungry."

"Actually, I am. Have you been up long?"

"A couple of hours. We'll come back to the room and pack after we eat. I figured we'd take a look at room ten, then head south. I've been thinking things over. It might be worth our time to stop off at the bar Tim got the matchbook from."

"That occurred to me as well. It's right on the highway, so it won't even be out of our way." I pulled a sweater over my blouse, then ran a brush through my hair. "I'm ready if you are."

The buffet was fantastic. There were chafing dishes with bacon, ham, and sausage, as well as three different egg dishes, home fries, toast, muffins, and wonderful-looking cinnamon rolls, and a choice of coffee, tea, hot cocoa, orange juice, and eggnog. I was going to need a long walk after I ate all the food I found myself piling onto my plate.

"I know we have a specific reason for being here, but I have to admit I'm enjoying the town and the inn. I'll have to come back when I can spend more time."

"It's very quaint," Shredder agreed.

I wasn't sure if Shredder meant that as a good thing or a bad one, but I supposed it didn't matter whether he enjoyed small-town life or not. He'd be gone in a few days and I'd probably never see him again.

"Did you find out anything more about Tim's activities prior to his death?" I asked, getting back on point.

"Based on the information available to me, I think it's likely Pickard is in Russia. I have people trying to narrow down the location. My plan is to spend today looking for the thumb drive, assuming there is one and Tim hadn't delivered it before he was killed. I'm hoping to find it, but either way, I leave tomorrow for Kotzebue. I hope to use Tim's being there as a jumping-off point to tracking down Pickard."

"Leave? But we haven't found Tim's killer yet."

"My mission was never to find Tim's killer per se; it was always to track down Pickard. In the beginning, I thought it was possible Pickard might have been the one to kill Tim. Now I don't think so."

"But what if he hired someone to kill him?" I argued.

Shredder cut his sausage link into small pieces. "He may very well have, but hired thugs are a dime a dozen. My goal is to find Pickard, and I doubt whoever he may have hired will be any more likely to lead me to him than Tim was."

I set down my fork and looked directly at Shredder. "I get the fact that you have bigger fish to fry, but if it turns out Pickard *is* in Russia, you only know that because of Tim. It seems to me you might owe him something."

"Perhaps. Tim's photo was the first lead I'd had in more than a year. And I'll help you as much as I can. But I have my orders. We have today to accomplish what we can, but I need to be on the road by dawn tomorrow. There'll be a plane waiting for me in

Fairbanks. Not showing up at the designated time isn't an option. I hope you understand."

I didn't but realized there was no point arguing. I wasn't happy Shredder wasn't going to stay until Tim's killer was found one way or another. But he'd come here to track down Pickard and his investigation, therefore, would most likely take him where the trail to the madman led.

******

When we arrived at room ten at ten o'clock we found it empty. The guests had checked out, but the maid hadn't yet been through. I figured we'd have maybe thirty minutes to look around before management would want it cleaned in preparation for whoever was checking in later.

"What are we looking for?" I asked.

"I'm not sure. I still don't know if Tim met his contact here in this room or if he left the drive hidden, where the person who checked in after him knew to look for it. We're still only guessing that whatever he was to hand off was a thumb drive, but given that Pickard deals in stolen information, it's a very good guess." Shredder opened and closed all the drawers in the dresser, running his hand along the bottom and sides of each one, as if looking for a hidden compartment.

"The hiding space wouldn't need to be very large, but it would have to be something the maid wouldn't stumble across. Did you find out who stayed here after Tim each time he was here?" I asked.

"I have a list, but the names and addresses don't bring up any red flags. I'm having my team take a closer look."

Shredder was running his hands over the walls so I went into the bathroom to look around. There was the usual sink, shower and tub combo, counter, and toilet. I knelt and examined everything as closely as possible but didn't find anything. I opened the cabinet under the sink and ran my hand over the decorative mirror. If Tim had a hiding place, it was well hidden.

I went back out to find Shredder standing in the center of the room with a frown on his face.

"No luck?" I asked.

"Not yet, but there has to be a reason Tim always asked for this room."

"This room can be used as a family suite," I pointed out. "There's a connecting door to the next room. Maybe he didn't leave anything behind after all. Maybe his contact stayed in the adjoining room."

Shredder raised a brow. "I guess it would be worth looking at. When we're done in here, I'll see who stayed in the adjoining room when Tim was here. I think a drop would be a better bet, but so far I haven't found a likely location." Shredder glanced around the room once again, frowned, and narrowed his gaze. Then he walked across the room to the fireplace and ran a hand along the mantel, stopping every so often to take a closer look at the wood beneath his hand. After a full minute, the face of one of the moose heads decorating the front popped open. "Well, lookee here. It seems our first suspicion might have been right after all."

The space behind the moose head was small, but not so tiny that a thumb drive couldn't be hidden there. When the head was closed, it didn't look at all different from its counterpart on the other side of the mantel. If you didn't know where to press to open the small compartment, you'd likely never stumble across it.

"I think we found our drop box," I said.

"Yeah. It's empty, which, because Tim never checked in that last time, is to be expected."

"Is it possible he stashed the drive in the hiding place and then someone picked it up much later? I know we're looking at whoever checked in immediately after Tim, but the hiding place is a good one. Someone could have come by for it at any time."

"Unless a name really pops, I doubt we'll figure out who picked it up. I'll get a list of everyone who's stayed in this room for the past three months. For now, let's pack our things, check out, and head for the bar."

The snow had stopped and a plow had been by, making the trip south a lot faster than the trip north had been. Shredder seemed deep in thought, so I put on my headphones and listened to music while we sped along the straight, flat road. I'd only known Shredder for a couple of days, but we'd delivered puppies together and I'd grown to like him. I was well aware that the people in your life were simply borrowed; even the ones closest to you could be gone at any moment. I tried not to get overly attached to anyone, especially those who didn't live in Rescue, but I'd miss my mysterious friend when he was gone.

It was lunchtime by the time we arrived at the bar, which, like Neverland, also served food, meaning the place was crowded at noon. We found a table in the corner and Shredder ordered us each a soda and a sandwich to share because we'd had such a big breakfast. When our order was placed, Shredder pulled the bartender aside. I could see he was showing the man the photo of Tim. I watched as the bartender nodded. Shredder handed him a folded bill, which I suspected was a hundred, and returned to the table.

"Bingo," Shredder said. "Tim was here the day before he was found dead. The bartender said he came in, used the bathroom, and left. He also said he'd been in a couple of other times over the past few months."

"So, we know he did head north that day; he just didn't make it to the inn. Do you think he arranged to meet his connection somewhere else?"

"Maybe," Shredder said. "Or maybe he hid the drive. The note he sent Harley indicated he had a plan. Maybe he was going to try to negotiate a deal of some sort using the drive as leverage."

"It could have happened that way. Maybe you should take a look around the bathroom. That's where the bartender said he was heading."

Shredder smiled. "I was just thinking the same thing."

While I waited, I checked my messages and returned a couple of texts to members of the animal shelter team, who were working on the remodel while I was busy chasing an international criminal. Shredder made it sound like Pickard had no alliances and would steal information from anyone. No wonder he found the need to stay hidden. It must be difficult to stay alive with so many enemies. Personally, I didn't understand the motivation for doing something like that. Sure, there was the money, but the guy was obviously a genius, and there were easier ways to make a buck. I supposed he might just like the challenge of hacking into the most well-secured databases in the world. It seemed like a waste to me, using his genius for evil, not good.

Shredder returned fifteen minutes later with a grin on his face.

"Did you find it?"

"I found it. Let's get out of here."

We still had another hour to go before we'd reach Rescue and I was about to settle in for another silent ride, but this time Shredder was chatty.

"I need to try to decrypt this to know what sort of information Tim had, but the fact that the drive hadn't been found could mean Pickard still has eyes in Rescue, just waiting for someone to come up with it. If he does, maybe we can lure them out. Either way, I'll put the word out that the drive has been retrieved before I leave. You should be safe once Pickard knows we have it."

"Isn't it a bad idea for you to let him know you're on to him before you find him?"

"Maybe. I'll talk to my superiors. Depending on what I find on the drive, we may need to come up with an alternate plan."

The rest of the drive was accomplished in silence. When he dropped me off, I asked Shredder if he wanted to come in, but he informed me that he needed to retrieve some things from the place he was staying. He asked if it would be okay if he left Riptide with me and came back for some dinner in a couple of hours. I told him Rescue didn't really have takeout places, though Sarge could box something up if he stopped by Neverland. He said he'd do it, and I headed into the house.

"You're back early," Justine said when I walked through the door, to be greeted by an entire pack of dogs.

"Weather cleared up, so it was a quick trip. How'd everything go?"

"Great. All the animals were fed this morning, but I hadn't gotten started on evening rounds yet. The pups have had two of their four meals. I was just about to give them the third. I've really grown attached to the chocolate-colored pup. He's a lot more alert than the others. I may even want to adopt him when he gets older, if that's okay."

"That would be great. I plan to find homes for all the puppies if I can. I already have quite the houseful."

"You really do. I took a drive out to the site for the shelter this morning. They have a lot done already. Having a place to take strays and unwanted pets is going to make a huge difference."

I felt my heart gladden. "Yeah. It really will."

Justine began to gather her things. "Oh, before I forget, someone called you. A man with a deep voice. I tried to take a message, but he didn't want to leave one. He said he'd call back, but I want to warn you, he sounded sort of creepy. Almost like he was talking through one of those voice-altering devices."

Well, that didn't sound good.

Chapter 12

Shredder arrived at around six with a bag from Neverland. He hadn't asked me what I wanted, but Jake and Sarge would be able to steer him in the right direction, so I wasn't worried. We decided to eat first, then discuss where we stood when we had some food in our stomachs. It seemed as if we'd done nothing but eat for the past twenty-four hours, yet I found I was hungry.

I knew I needed to tell Shredder about the creepy call Justine had taken for me, but I figured I'd wait until after we ate. I'd fed, exercised, and tended to all the animals after she left, so all I had to do was give the pups their final supplemental meal of the day and I'd be free the rest of the evening.

"So, do you have a home? A place you go when you aren't on the road chasing bad guys?" I asked.

Shredder nodded. "I have a place. I can't say where; it doesn't matter."

"I guess with all the traveling you do, it makes it hard to have things in your life like plants or a girlfriend."

"I tried to have a plant once. The woman at the nursery assured me it didn't need a lot of water or attention, but it died during the first assignment I had after I got it. I have Riptide, however, and I do have friends who have grown to mean a lot to me despite the fact that I'll very likely be moving on before long."

"You must enjoy what you do or you wouldn't do it, but it sounds lonely. Do you have to relocate often?"

"More often than I'd like."

"Have you ever thought about doing something else? Something a bit more structured, where you wouldn't have to travel so much?"

Shredder shrugged. "Sometimes. In the end, I'd be bored with a nine-to-five gig. I may not have chosen the life I have, but it suits me. How about you? Do you ever think of leaving Rescue and seeing the world?"

"No. Not at all. I love it here. My friends and animals are here. I can't imagine ever wanting to leave, no matter what the reason."

I was about to ask Shredder about hobbies when my house phone rang. I got up, walked across the room, and answered it.

"Is this Harmony Carson?" a deep voice asked.

"Who is this?"

"It doesn't matter. I'm looking for something Tim Maverick had before he died. I wonder if he might have left it with you."

I made eye contact with Shredder, trying to relay that the call I was on could be an important one. "I barely knew Tim. There's no reason for him to have left anything with me."

"You've been asking around about his activities before his death. That doesn't sound like something a woman who barely knew someone would do."

"I was helping a friend find some answers, but we came up empty. I need to go." I hung up before the man could reply.

"What was that all about?" Shredder asked.

I explained about the call Justine had taken while I was away, as well as this one. "He had a deep, strange voice. Like he was calling from a tunnel. There was a distinct echo."

Shredder frowned. "I'm not liking this one bit. I have some equipment in my vehicle. I'm going to get it in case he calls back. If the phone rings before I get back, don't answer it."

"Okay." The look on Shredder's face had me concerned. I consider myself to be a brave person generally. I don't mean spy brave, but I'm not easily intimidated. Still, with everything that was going on, I felt my stomach churn and my mouth grow dry.

Shredder hooked my phone up to his equipment, then had a conversation with whoever he was always checking in with. I listened while he explained about the phone tap and what he was trying to accomplish. Once everything was hooked up, he turned to look at me. "The phone now has both a tap and a tracer. What that means is that any conversation you have will be recorded, so you may want to use your cell for personal calls. If the man calls back, we'll try to trace the call to its source."

"Do you think I'm in danger?"

"If it's Pickard and he believes you have the drive or know where it is, yes."

"Should we call the police?"

"No. I'll stay with you tonight. I don't suppose you have any sort of alarm system?"

"Does seven barking dogs count?"

Shredder lifted an eyebrow. "Actually, yes. If you need to go out to the barn or take the dogs out, I'll go with you. Do you still have that shotgun you pulled on me?"

"I do."

"Is it loaded?"

"Always."

Shredder looked around, then glanced at the computer he'd set up on my dining table. "We've done what we can. Now, let's see if we can get the drive decrypted. The sooner we know what's on it, the sooner we can leak the fact that we have it and the sooner you'll no longer be in danger."

I'll admit I'm not a whiz on the computer, and Shredder seemed like he knew what he was doing, so I sat back and watched him work. If he ended up needing help, we could call Landon, who was a genius when it came to anything cyber. I wasn't only amazed at the look of complete focus and concentration on Shredder's face but the speed with which his tanned fingers flew over the keyboard. I could navigate cyberspace all right, but I'd never had much of an interest in learning how to go beyond the basics. I did, however, admire people with the intelligence and patience to do so.

It looked like Shredder was settled in for the long haul, so I decided to let Honey out and then give the pups their last meal of the day. Shredder didn't want me going out alone, but all I intended to do was stand on the back porch while the dog did her business and then come right back in. The rest of my pack would need a bit longer in the yard, so once I fed the pups, Shredder could come out with me if he really felt he needed to.

Once she was outside, Honey looked toward the denseness of the woods and growled.

"What is it, girl? Do you see something?"

She didn't move toward the woods, but she didn't return to me either.

"Maybe we should go inside. Your babies need their dinner."

Honey glanced at me, then back toward the woods. She barked loudly several times before coming in my direction. It was possible there was a bear in the woods. Although most would be in hibernation by now, there were a few stragglers every year. And it wouldn't be unheard of to have a moose or even a wolf in the yard. I had to be extra careful to keep the barn locked so wolves couldn't get in and make a meal of Homer, who had no way to defend himself.

Back in the house, I mixed up the formula and prepared four bottles. A quick peek in the living area confirmed Shredder was still bent over his computer. I had two guest rooms, but neither had been cleaned in a while, so I'd need to prepare one for him when I'd finished with the pups if he really did plan to stay over.

Other than Jake, I'd never had a man spend the night in my house. Of course, it wasn't like Shredder was actually *spending the night*. I did feel better, though, knowing he'd be close by if the goon from the phone call was in the area and posed a threat to me.

I'd just finished feeding puppy number two when the phone rang. I set the pup down next to Honey and went into the living room. Shredder motioned for me to pick up the phone.

"Hello."

"It seems we may have been cut off the last time I called," the man with the deep voice said.

"Yes," I answered. "I'm afraid that's what happened. I didn't have much to add to what I'd already said, however. I barely knew Tim and he absolutely didn't leave anything with me."

"Don't lie to me," the deep, garbled voice shouted. "I'd hate to get blood all over your pretty blue sweater."

I paled. I was wearing a blue sweater.

"I'm not lying," I answered. "Tim didn't give me anything. I really can't help you."

"You have a guest. Who is it?"

I glanced at Shredder. He shook his head.

"My boyfriend," I answered. "We're having dinner."

"Does your boyfriend know anything about the item Tim left?"

"No," I assured the man. "My boyfriend is new to town. He never even met Tim. Have you tried looking at Tim's cabin for whatever it is you're after?"

"It's not there. I need to go now, but remember, I'm watching you." He hung up.

"Can you trace it?" I asked.

"He hung up too soon. The guy must suspect we were tracing the call."

I glanced at the window. The drape was open, but I had a sudden urge to close it, and all the other ones in the house too. "He knows you're here. Do you think he knows who you are?"

Shredder glanced at the window himself, then got up and closed the drape himself. "I don't think so. I operate under deep cover. If he can see us, he must be nearby. I doubt it's Pickard, but it could be one of his thugs. Go around and make sure all the doors and windows are locked and the drapes are closed."

"The dogs will need to go out again."

Shredder pulled a gun out of the pocket of the jacket hanging on the peg at the front door. "I'll take them. Lock the door behind me and only open it if I knock three times, followed by a pause, and then a single rap."

"Okay."

"Even if I say, 'Hey, it's me, let me in,' don't open up without the knock."

"Okay."

"Promise me."

"I promise."

"Are the animals in the barn okay?"

I nodded. "I saw to them already."

Shredder called all the dogs except for Honey and headed to the door. I locked it behind him. It was awfully cold tonight. If there was someone lingering in the woods, I didn't think they'd be able to stay there for long.

The phone rang again, but I let it go to the answering machine. Whoever it was didn't leave a message. Every minute Shredder was outdoors seemed like an hour. I needed to finish feeding the pups, but there was no way I could take my eyes off the door until Shredder returned. I almost jumped out of my skin when my cell rang. I ignored that too. Whoever it was could wait.

After what seemed like an eternity, Shredder knocked and I let him in. He checked all the locks, then went back to the computer. I went into the bedroom to feed the last two pups. I was just finishing up when I heard Shredder yell, "Got it." I joined him in the living room to see he was frowning at the computer.

"Did you get in?" I asked.

"Yeah."

"And…?"

"And it's not good. It looks like Pickard planned to sell a list with the aliases and current locations of more than a dozen CIA operatives."

"But we stopped it, right? Or, more precisely, Tim stopped it?"

"It's more like Tim *delayed* it. Pickard stole the information once. He can steal it again. We need to find him and put an end to his reign of terror once and for all. In the meantime, the CIA will recall the operatives at risk."

Shredder turned back to his computer. He began typing in commands, so I assumed our conversation was over. I wasn't sure what would come next, but I hadn't been much more than a passenger for this entire ride.

"Who do you think has been calling? The person who was supposed to receive the drive?"

"Probably. It should be assumed he's armed and dangerous. And that he'll stop at nothing to get the drive. The sooner we can get the word out that it's decrypted, the better. Once everyone involved knows it's worthless, whoever is after it will move on."

It sounded like we just needed to stay holed up in the house until the person who wanted the drive realized the CIA had been notified of the contents and had acted to neutralize it. I was a little surprised that if there really was someone in the woods behind the house, they didn't just storm the place. It could be Honey had simply been growling at an animal and whoever was watching us was doing so remotely. The other dogs hadn't gone crazy when Shredder had taken them out, and if there'd been someone nearby, Denali, especially, would have had him for dinner.

Shredder was busy, so I picked up my cell and checked for messages. There was one from Jake, letting me know they had a rescue underway and could really use my help.

"I need to go," I said aloud.

"Go? Go where?"

"Jake needs me. There's a rescue."

Shredder paused, then said, "I don't think it's a good idea to leave the house."

"I can't just ignore a person in need."

"It could be a trap."

"A trap? What sort of trap?"

"Maybe your caller wants to smoke us out so we'll leave the house. We'll be more vulnerable when we're on the road. The dogs will alert us if anyone approaches the house, and we have guns and ammunition. I say we stay here."

"But…"

"No buts," Shredder said. "If Jake knew the situation, he'd agree."

Shredder was right. If Jake did know what was going on, he would agree.

"You were able to connect to the girl whose family was in the accident while we were on the road. That means you don't have to be at the bar or with the team to help them. Get whoever's in charge on the phone. Tell them you're sick, but you're happy to help. Get the information you need and try to do it from here."

I supposed that might work. I could get a connection, if I was meant to, from anywhere. I called Jake, who told me the victims were two missing kids, aged twelve and thirteen, both boys. He didn't have a lot of information other than that he'd received a call from a man who said the boys had gone shooting earlier in the day and weren't back at the house at the time they'd arranged.

"What are their names?" I asked.

"Peter and Kevin," Jake informed me. "Wyatt, Landon, and I are going to take a look around on the snowmobiles. We have no idea where to begin looking, though, so unless you're able to connect, I don't know what we can do. Sarge will monitor you on the phone."

"Okay. I'll do what I can."

I sat down and closed my eyes. I tried to focus my energy on the names Jake had given me, but I was coming up empty. "Do you have any other information?" I asked Sarge.

"No. Just the names and ages. The man hung up before Jake could get more. He tried to call him back, but he didn't answer."

I relaxed my body and focused on the names. I tried to see the boys in my head, but there was nothing. After ten minutes, I picked up the phone again. "I'm sorry. I've got nothing."

"It was kind of a strange call," Sarge admitted. "When Jake filled me in on the specifics, I almost wondered if it was a prank."

I hesitated. We'd received prank calls in the past, and it very well could be my caller, trying to smoke me out. "Do you have the number the call was made from?"

"Should have it. Hang on." Sarge came back on the line a minute later. "The number's blocked."

"Call Jake and the others back in. I've gotten a couple of prank calls at the house tonight as well. It seems someone with a very unfunny sense of humor is trying to pull my leg."

"Are you sure?"

"I'm sure. When I tried to connect, there was nothing at all. Not an image just out of reach, or a sense that I was close. There was simply nothing. That's never happened before. If you do get additional information that leads you to believe the rescue is real, call me back. I'll keep the phone nearby."

"Okay, Harm. Let's hope you're right."

Yeah, I thought to myself, *let's hope I am*. I glanced at Shredder, who was staring at me. "It looks like you were right. Someone just wanted us out of the house." I took a deep breath. "Are we going to be okay?"

"We'll be okay. Trust me; I won't let anything happen to you."

I trusted Shredder, but it was very unnerving to know there was someone out there who might very well threaten my life. Shredder sat back down at the computer and I went into a guest room to change the bedding and clean up a bit. Denali, who I sensed was picking up on my tension, followed me into the room. All my dogs were protective of me to a certain degree, but I knew if I was ever really threatened by a madman with a gun, Denali wouldn't hesitate to attack. I just hoped he wasn't injured in the crossfire.

Once I was satisfied the guest room was as clean as it was going to be, I wandered into my own room. I had just opened the closet to hang up the sweater I'd worn that day when I heard a sound outside my window. Denali launched into attack mode and ran to the window. He put his front paws on the sill and barked aggressively at whoever or whatever was outside.

Shredder came running into the room with Riptide and the other dogs on his heels. "What is it?"

"I don't know. I heard a noise, a thunking sort of sound, and then Denali went berserk."

Shredder grabbed the gun he'd tucked into the back of his belt. "Stay here and away from the window. I'll check it out."

"No! Don't go outside. If it's the caller, he probably has a gun. It's safer in here."

"I'll sneak out the front and circle around to the back. I'll be fine. Wait here for me."

My heart literally skipped a beat when Shredder left the room. I hadn't been quite this scared since the night Val had gone missing. Riptide was standing at the door, Denali was still looking out the window, where Shia had joined him, and Honey and Lucky were sitting at my feet. I was too scared to breathe as I waited for whatever was going to happen.

"Get a grip," I whispered to myself.

I took several deep breaths, then refocused my fear on survival. I knew Shredder had told me to wait, but waiting wasn't my strong suit. I scratched Honey and Lucky behind the ears in an offer of comfort, then went for my rifle. I pulled on my black parka and tucked my hair up under a black ski cap. I motioned for the dogs to be quiet as I snuck out the front door. I suspected Shredder had already circled around to the back, so I went in that direction.

When I got there, I saw Shredder standing with his pistol drawn at the edge of the clearing. He was looking in to the woods, although I couldn't figure out how he could see anything. It was totally dark and he didn't have a flashlight. I was about to step toward him when I noticed a movement on the rocky ledge behind where he was standing. I barely had a chance to get off a shot before the shadow leaped from the height of the ledge in preparation to attack Shredder from behind.

"What the hell?" He spun around and looked at me when he heard the shot.

"Cougar."

Shredder looked behind him and then started walking in my direction. "Cougar?"

"He was stalking you from behind. Lesson number one when walking around in the dark in Alaska: watch your back. Living all the way out here, I get a lot of wildlife."

"Is he dead?"

I shook my head. "I shot over his head. It scared him away, but he's still probably nearby. Let's get inside."

"I guess I understand why you carry that rifle everywhere you go."

"I rarely leave the house without it."

Shredder started back toward the house and I fell in beside him. "I thought I told you to stay inside."

"You're welcome."

"Don't get me wrong, I'm grateful you probably just saved my life, but I'm not used to having my orders ignored."

"I'm not on your team and I'm not one of your men, so I don't need to obey you," I pointed out. "Besides, I'm famous for rarely doing as I'm told."

Shredder grinned. "Good to know."

Chapter 13

Tuesday, December 19

Shredder stayed an extra day to be sure Pickard knew the drive had been found and decrypted. His team felt they were closing in on him, so as quickly as he appeared in my life, he left. The calls from the man with the deep voice had stopped and the dogs weren't showing any signs that there was anyone lurking in the woods. Shredder ordered me to keep my blinds drawn and the windows and doors locked at all times. He also told me to take my rifle with me when I went outdoors, which we both knew I did anyway. I hadn't seen the cougar again, but I'd heard wolves at night and knew they were close.

Shredder programed a number where I could reach him into my cell phone and told me to use it in case of emergency only. I doubted I'd have an emergency I needed his help with, and I also doubted I'd ever see him again. I wasn't sure what to do about finding Tim's killer at this point. Assuming he'd been murdered and hadn't simply OD'd, as the police thought, it didn't look like Pickard was his killer. And if not Pickard, who did that leave? Deep voice? Someone else entirely?

Harley was coming back to Rescue this evening and we'd made plans to have dinner and catch up. In the meantime, I wanted to go over to the shelter to check in with the team there, and I needed to go to Neverland to check in with Jake. We'd never determined a date for me to return to my regular shift. The stipend Shredder had worked out for me exceeded the amount of money I'd make in two months at the bar, so if Jake didn't need me, I wouldn't mind taking a few extra days off.

"Anyone here?" I said as I walked in through the front door of the bar.

"In the back," Jake called from the storeroom. He stopped what he was doing and looked up when I walked in. "Look what the cat dragged in. Was your trip successful?"

"Sort of. We managed to wrap up the project Shredder was in town for, but Harley and I still need to find Tim's killer."

Jake set the box he'd opened to one side and began slitting the top of the next one in the stack. "I thought the man you and Shredder were after were one and the same."

I leaned a hip against the counter. "We thought so as well, but it turns out we were wrong. Shredder accomplished what he wanted to, so he took off early this morning."

"Is he coming back?"

"Probably not. But Harley's is coming back tonight, and I'd like to help him figure out what happened to Tim. The consultant's fee Shredder worked out for me was more than enough to cover my earnings for the time I was gone and then some, so if you don't need me, I'd like to take the rest of the week off."

"Fine by me. Sally's home for Christmas break and happy to make a few bucks before she heads back to college. I'm sure she'll cover for you for as long as you want."

I smiled. "Great. I also want to help out with the shelter, so that works perfectly."

Jake picked up one of the boxes he'd just opened and headed toward the bar. "So, how's the remodel going?"

"Considering it's only been a little more than a week, fantastic. I stopped by before coming here, and the team's already putting up walls and mapping out cages. If we keep our motivation up, I see no reason we can't be open by spring. At least with phase one."

"Phase one?"

"If we can work out something with Kelly or another veterinarian in the area, I'd eventually like to expand to wild animal rescue and rehabilitation, but for now, a place for homeless dogs and cats will be totally awesome."

"I have to hand it to you," Jake said as he stacked rum bottles on a shelf. 'You set a goal for yourself and stuck with it."

I leaned my head to the side. "I suppose it *was* my idea to build the shelter, but we'd still be at ground zero if not for Harley."

"Maybe, but if not for your drive to see it through, the project would have died a long time ago."

I shrugged. "Maybe."

I poured myself a glass of water and slid onto a stool while Jake continued to stock inventory. "We haven't really talked about Christmas. Do you want to come to my place?"

"Actually," Jake said, "I thought we might decorate the bar. I plan to close after the lunch crowd clears out on Christmas Eve and then not reopen until regular time on the twenty-sixth, so I thought we could make dinner for everyone here. I asked the others when they were here last night and they were all for it."

"That sounds fun. Is Jordan off?"

Jake went back into the storeroom to get another box before he responded. "She's on call, but unless she has an emergency, she's off. Landon, Wyatt, and Austin all said they had nowhere to go. Dani has a date, but she said if it's okay for her to bring him with her, she'd come as well. Chloe has family in town, but if she's free, you can invite her as well."

"Okay, I'll ask her." I looked around the bar. "We'll need a tree."

"Landon volunteered to get one, but if you have some time this afternoon, it might be a good idea if you went with him. I love the guy like a brother, but he doesn't seem to notice the small details in everyday life. I'm afraid we'll end up with a Charlie Brown tree."

I laughed. "I'd be happy to go with him."

******

Landon Stanford is the sort of person one might refer to as a nerd. As far as men in general go, he isn't bad-looking in comparison to most, and some might even consider his tall frame, dark hair, and dark eyes attractive. He's extremely intelligent, with an IQ that's supposed to be off the charts. It's occurred to me on more than one occasion that he should be working for the government or some big technology firm. Instead, he does freelance work out of his small cabin in Rescue. I suspect there's a story behind the fact that he seems to be hiding from the world, but so far, he hasn't been inclined to tell me what it is.

Landon had joined the team shortly after Val died. Jake admitted he wasn't sure he could handle the physical demands the team required, but over the years, Landon has proven again and again that he was more than just a brilliant brain and a pretty smile. He'd logged as many hours as anyone else and had never missed a step while doing so. Landon might be an enigma, but he was a good friend, and I trusted him with my life. He may not be as funny and charming as Wyatt, as classically good-looking as Austin, or as friendly and welcoming as Jake, but despite his quiet approach to life, and his introverted and sometimes awkward ways, I could guarantee that in a crisis, he was exactly the man you would want in your corner.

"I'm sure there's a logical solution to your problem," Landon said as we trod through knee-deep snow in search of the perfect tree.

"It would seem, but we've hit a dead end. I really thought Pickard killed Tim. Tim as much as said so himself. But Shredder is fairly certain Pickard has never been in Rescue, and if he'd killed Tim, he would have just shot him instead of taking the time to stage a suicide or accident. Tim could have been killed by one of Pickard's thugs, but if that were true,

I imagine they're long gone and therefore out of our reach."

"Maybe you need to look at the situation from a different angle."

I called Shia to my side before I answered. We'd brought all six of my dogs along with Sitka with us, so we had a full pack to keep track of. "What do you mean, a different angle?"

"As far as I know, you've been operating under the assumption that Tim was killed because of his job as a courier for the man in the photo."

"Yes. That's because Tim told us he would be the one to do it."

Landon looked down at his compass, then continued walking. "You said Shredder suggested that if Pickard or one of his men killed Tim, they would have just shot him, and I agree. Men who kill for a living don't take the time to stage a killing to look like an accident. Additionally, dying from a heroin overdose seems personal, given the fact that Tim was a recovering drug addict. My bet is, Tim was killed by someone who knew him well."

I stopped and looked at Landon, who was dressed in a forest-green sweater perfect for the task at hand. "Well, that's grim. It was bad enough believing Tim was killed by some nameless thug, but a friend? Who would do such a thing?"

Landon ran his hands over the fir tree he'd paused to check for freshness. "I don't know. It seems the first step would be to speak to the people who knew him best to see if they noticed anything going on with Tim other than the new courier job. Was he dating? Did he have a new friend in his life? Had he been hanging out with his old drug buddies? Did he owe someone money? The list can go on and on, but you get the idea."

It took me a minute to really understand what Landon was saying, but when I did, I realized he had a good point. We'd been focusing on one suspect and one suspect only. Assuming Tim was murdered and hadn't simply OD'd, were there other people who might have had motive to kill him? A drug dealer he'd stiffed in the past? A girl whose heart he'd broken? Someone he owed a debt? Considering he'd sent the photo to Harley and he ended up dead the day after hiding the drive, it seemed unlikely but not impossible.

"I get what you're saying, but I do think looking for a killer with another motive given the timing of the other events could be a waste of time. Is there any reason you're suggesting we do so?"

"One thing I've learned in my life is never to get so focused on a single assumption that you miss everything else. As long as you've hit a dead end in your search, I don't see the harm in at least thinking about other options. You may learn something important along the way."

I supposed Landon could be right.

"What do you think about this one?" he asked with a grin on his face. It was times like this that he seemed more human and less robotic.

"I like it. It's tall and full but not too wide. It's perfect. Did you bring an ax?"

Landon had a panicked look on his face.

I grinned and reached into my pack. "I brought one just in case."

Landon chopped down the tree while I called the dogs back. They were pretty good about staying within yelling range, but I didn't want anyone getting lost, especially with a storm brewing. I looked up into the sky and calculated the amount of time we had before we were hit head-on.

"Two hours and twenty-six minutes," Landon said as he walked up beside me with the tree on the sled behind him.

"Until…?"

"Until the storm gets here. It took us fifty-three minutes to walk from my truck here. We'll need to tow the tree on the way back, but we've worn a trail that will make the going easier. Still, I predict it will take sixty-eight minutes to return. The drive to Jake's place to pick up the ornaments will take twenty-six minutes, and then we'll need another ten to load up and eight minutes more to reach the bar. That's a total of one hundred and twelve minutes. We have thirty-four minutes to spare."

Landon the human calculator was back. "I need to stop by my house, drop off the dogs, and feed the pups."

"Then we'd better get going instead of standing around talking."

Chapter 14

I couldn't help but grin when I walked into Neverland later that evening and saw Harley waiting for me. I'd missed him a lot more than I'd wanted to. I guess I'd always been attracted to him, and his welcoming smile caused little butterflies in my stomach the way no other man's ever had, but he lived in LA and I lived in Alaska, so pursuing any attraction we might share could only lead to heartache and shattered dreams.

"You're early," I said as Harley got up and pulled out my chair, then kissed me on the cheek after I'd been seated.

"I was bored sitting at the inn, so I decided to come into town to do some shopping. I've only been at the bar for about ten minutes," Harley answered as he walked back around the table and took his chair. "The place looks really nice."

"Doesn't it? Landon and I cut the tree this afternoon and then the whole gang stopped by to help decorate it. Dani used the extra branches to make the garland for the mantel, and Wyatt helped Jordan with all the red bows. It feels very Christmassy. Which reminds me: we're all having Christmas Eve dinner here in the bar. Jake is closing it to the public. If you're still in town, you should come."

"I'd like that."

I waved to Jake, who started in my direction carrying a rum and Coke.

"You guys ready to order?" Jake asked.

Harley and I both settled on the pot roast with baby carrots and potatoes. Jake went back to the bar, which was my cue to catch Harley up on things. I began by providing a condensed version of everything that had occurred while he was away, including the trip Shredder and I had taken up north, our discovery of the thumb drive, the calls from the man with the deep voice, and Shredder's conclusion that Pickard had most likely never been in Rescue.

"So where does that leave us in terms of Tim's death?" Harley asked the same question I'd been asking myself all day.

"I've given this some thought. The first possibility is that Shredder was wrong and Pickard *was* in Rescue, and he killed Tim because he failed to deliver the drive. That seems like the simplest answer because Tim himself told you Pickard would be the one who was responsible if something happened to him, but Shredder struck me as the sort of guy who's good at his job and knows the players as well as anyone can. While I wouldn't completely eliminate Pickard, Shredder made a good argument that the man who stays alive due to his ability to remain invisible probably never left Russia, or wherever it is he's been hiding."

"I guess that makes sense," Harley agreed.

"And then we need to consider someone connected to Pickard: either the buyer who came away empty-handed or one of Pickard's thugs killed Tim on Pickard's behalf. The fact that Tim's home was tossed seems to support the idea that Tim was killed because of his failure to deliver the drive and then someone ransacked his cabin attempting to find it."

"That does sound like a good theory," Harley answered.

"I agree. However, Landon had another perspective I think we would be remiss not to consider. He pointed out that if Tim had been killed by someone who did it for a living, he most likely would have been shot. Killing Tim, a former drug addict who'd worked very hard to get clean for a lot of years, seemed personal."

"Another good point."

"Landon reasoned that given the method of his death, Tim was most likely killed by someone who knew him well and wanted to make a statement."

Harley slowly nodded his head. "That does make sense. But what are the odds that Tim would steal a valuable item from an international criminal and then be killed by someone completely unrelated the following day?"

"It would be very low odds indeed. But not impossible."

"Okay, so if someone from Tim's personal life not related to his job as a courier killed him, who tossed the house? The killer or the thugs looking for the thumb drive?"

I shrugged. "At this point, I don't think we can know."

"So what are you suggesting?"

I sat back in my chair and organized my thoughts before I spoke. "By now, Pickard, the buyer, and Pickard's thugs all know the drive has been recovered by Shredder and his people. If they were in Alaska, and if they did kill Tim, they'd probably be long gone by now. The chance of you and me doing anything to avenge Tim's death seems pretty unlikely. However, if Tim was killed by an ex-lover, a drug dealer, someone he owed money to, or someone he simply pissed off, we may be dealing with an ordinary person going about their life, thinking they got away with murder. If that's the case, our odds of figuring out who's responsible are a whole lot better."

"So, you're suggesting we conduct the investigation we're more likely to have success with."

"Exactly. My sense is that Shredder is getting close to tracking down Pickard. If he catches up with him, I have a feeling he'll get the answers he's after one way or another. If that happens, he might eventually be able to answer questions about Tim, if Pickard does turn out to be the one responsible. In the meantime, I think you and I should cover the home front."

"Who exactly does this Shredder work for?" Harley asked.

"Hell if I know. He's a slippery, secretive sort, but I spent enough time with him to be sure he's one of the good guys."

After Harley and I finished our dinner, we made plans for the following day. He was still staying at the inn, so I'd pick him up there after I finished my morning chores.

The first thing I did when I got home that night was take all the dogs out for a bathroom break. It was pitch black by then and it had begun to snow, so I grabbed a flashlight and my rifle, though I planned to stay within sight of the back-porch light. The fact that the cougar still seemed to be around made me more than just a little cautious.

I decided after I saw to all the animals, I'd make a list of people Harley and I should talk to. I'd already spoken to Jared Martin, the pharmacist, Teresa Toller, the woman it was reported Tim had been dating, and Gill Greenland at the gas station, but they all seemed like good people to chat with a second time in the hope of learning something new. Because Tim had been killed overdosing on heroin, it might also be a good idea to find out who would have access to the drug. As far as I knew, heroin wasn't widely distributed in Rescue. I supposed the police could provide additional information about the drug trade and culture in town, if we could get them to talk to us.

Mary from the inn also had mentioned Tim had been going to church. A chat with the pastor might tell us something.

"Come on back, everyone," I called into the night. The last thing I wanted was for anyone to wander too far away with a cougar around.

All the dogs came back except Shia, who, at times, had a mind of her own.

"Shia, come," I called.

I could hear a rustling in the nearby woods and hoped it was her and not a predator.

"Now," I called in my sternest voice.

Luckily, that did it; Shia poked her nose out from behind a bush.

"Home," I commanded, and all the dogs took off in that direction.

I dropped the house dogs off there and headed to the barn with Juno and Kodi. It took a while to take care of everyone's needs, and I felt something of an urgency to get back to the house to see to the puppies, but I hadn't spent a lot of time with Homer lately, and I knew that even though he couldn't see me, he missed me.

I talked to the animals as I cleaned the stalls and freshened water. It was my opinion that all the animals, even the rabbits, responded to the sound of my voice. I think it made them feel cared for and included.

I was sure to lock up the barn behind me so the predators couldn't get in. By the time I got back to the house, the house dogs and cats were standing somewhat impatiently in front of their empty bowls. I fed everyone and changed out cat litter and water, then went into the bedroom to see to the puppies.

It was late by the time I'd taken care of everyone and I realized I'd never gotten around to making my list. I considered leaving it for the morning, but I knew if I didn't get my thoughts down on paper I'd lay awake trying to remember everything I wanted to be certain I wouldn't forget.

I tossed another log on the fire, then grabbed a pen and a pad. I was pretty sure I had wine stashed in the back of one of my cupboards, so I searched through and found it and poured myself a glass. I put a Christmas CD on the stereo and clicked on the colored lights I'd hung around the place. Once I was cozied up under a quilt I kept on the sofa, I started my list.

The first three names I wrote down were Jared Martin, Teresa Toller, and Gill Greenland. Under Gill's name I wrote Pastor Brown, and below him I added Eddy Halverson. Eddy and Tim had been friends back when he was using, though I knew he'd broken off his relationship with him when he decided to get clean. As far as I knew, Eddy still dabbled, mostly with marijuana, but it was possible he'd have some insight into the who's who of the local drug culture.

After I wrote down Eddy's name, I paused, clicking my pen open and closed as I considered other options. It would be easier to come up with a more comprehensive list if Tim and I had been better friends, but although I'd seen him around town from time to time, we never really stopped to chat.

Juno and Kodi started barking, and I paused to listen. They didn't usually bark unless a predator was near. I doubted that either a cougar or a coyote could get into the barn, but a bear could if we happened to have a boar who was late to go into hibernation. However unlikely it was, I decided I should check.

Of course, once I got up, all the dogs got up too, but I told them to stay. I turned on the porch light and listened. I didn't hear anything, but I grabbed my gun and took a step onto the back stoop. I could see the path from the house to the barn was clear, but I fired a warning shot into the air, then waited. I gave it a minute, and when I didn't see or hear anything, I walked slowly toward the barn. I arrived and paused, looking at the prints in the snow. I gasped when I realized last night's intruder hadn't been a bear but a human who'd left fairly large boot prints behind.

"Is anyone there?" I called.

No one answered and I didn't see anyone, so I returned to the house. Inside, I made sure all the doors and windows were locked, then went to bed. I slept with my rifle loaded and next to the bed that whole night, something I hadn't done in a very long time.

Chapter 15

Wednesday, December 20

Despite the late start of the night before, I slept fairly well and woke up early. I made quick work of my morning chores because I wanted to pick Harley up at the inn by around ten so we'd have plenty of time before I needed to meet Chloe for the cookie exchange. She'd insisted I participate, even though I didn't have the first clue how to bake cookies. When I pointed that out to her, she'd agreed to make a batch of cookies for me as well as herself.

I still had no idea who'd been lurking around the barn last night, but the dogs hadn't picked up a scent when I'd taken them out this morning, so I had to assume whoever it had been was long gone. I took the dogs for a long walk this morning, knowing I would be out for a good part of the day while they'd be cooped up inside.

I'd spotted a cute little fir when I'd been out and wondered if I should get a tree for my house. I would be spending Christmas with Jake and didn't usually bother, but this year I was feeling extra festive. Of course, if I got a tree I'd need to buy some lights, which I was sure I could easily find in town.

Harley was ready and waiting when I arrived at the inn. I thought we might sit a spell and firm up our list, but he'd made an appointment with a local Realtor and needed to leave right away.

"Are you buying some property?" I asked as I followed the directions he was feeding me.

"I'm looking at a house. I hadn't realized how much I missed Rescue until I came home after all this time. I travel a lot for work, but I have a lot of time off as well, so I decided I'd like to spend at least part of that time in Rescue."

"That's wonderful." I grinned.

"I was lucky to find this house. I hope it's as perfect for my needs as it sounded in the ad. I have a movie to film right after the first of the year, but then I'm obligation-free for the remainder of the year. I think I'll keep it that way. I need some time off to reevaluate my life. Not that it's a bad life, but I've been doing one movie after another for so long that I feel as if I've lost the part of who I am who isn't an actor along the way. Make a left at the next road."

The house Harley led me to turned out to be a large ranch that had been built on the side of a hill. I was sure it must have a beautiful view from every window, but keeping the long private drive plowed was going to be a challenge. Of course, Harley was rich, so I imagined he could hire someone to see to that.

"Wow. This is really something," I gasped as I got out and looked around.

"It does seem pretty perfect. The Realtor should be waiting inside. The best part about the house, other than the view, is that it's being sold completely furnished, which means I can start using it right away. In fact, if my offer is accepted, I plan to pay cash so I can move right in as soon as I finish filming."

The first thing I noticed when we walked through the front door was the open floor plan. The main living area faced a wall of windows that looked out over the entire valley. Behind that was a huge kitchen I was willing to bet my entire house would fit inside. The house had four bedrooms and five baths, plus a formal dining room and a game room complete with a pool table and home theater system. It was spectacular, but I couldn't imagine why one person would even want such a huge space.

Of course, I was just assuming Harley would be alone. I hadn't asked about his love life, mostly because it was none of my business and I didn't want to know, but I knew he dated often, so it stood to reason his time in Rescue would be in the company of his girlfriend of the moment.

I wandered around the house as Harley and the Realtor discussed the details. On one hand, I found Harley to be a warm and friendly person I'd very much welcome into my life. On the other, witnessing Harley's parade of women up close and personal might be more than my poor heart could take. When he was in LA and I was here, I rarely gave him a second thought, but in the brief time he'd been in Rescue, I'd definitely given him a third and a fourth.

When I returned to the room where he and the Realtor were talking, I heard mention of Tim's name. I didn't want it to seem like I was listening in, so I headed out onto the deck to take in the whole view. It was a tolerable temperature today, so I was able to enjoy the fresh air without freezing to death despite my heavy parka and sturdy snow boots.

"Are you all set?" I asked when Harley and the Realtor joined me on the deck.

"For now," Harley answered.

"Expect to find the contract in your email within the next two hours. Once you sign it electronically, send it back and I'll forward it to the owner."

"I'll watch for it, and thank you for meeting us."

"No problem. I look forward to having you back in the community."

The Realtor drove away and Harley and I piled back into my Jeep.

"I'll need to buy a sturdy four-wheel drive I can just leave here."

"It would be a good idea, especially with that driveway. You're either going to need to buy a plow or you'll have to hire someone to take care of it for you."

"I've driven a plow, but I'll need to pay someone to keep the road clear while I'm out of town."

I pulled onto the main highway back toward Rescue. "So, where do you want to start?"

"I mentioned to the Realtor that I'd initially come to town after Tim passed away, and she mentioned he spent a lot of time at a bar south of town called Gremlins."

"A bar? I thought he was sober."

"She said he was. The bar has pool tables and he'd go there to play pool with some of his old friends."

"Sounds to me like he was playing with fire."

Harley shrugged. "Perhaps. But it might be worth our while to talk to the bartender. You never know when someone might have noticed something no one else did."

Gremlins was nothing like Neverland. Neverland was a warm, cozy community meeting place that served quality drinks and delicious food. It was clean and welcoming and had plenty of windows to let in as much natural light as you were likely to get in this part of the state, at least in the winter. Gremlins was dark and depressing, with nary a window in sight. There were tables and chairs on one side of the room and several pool tables on the other. I couldn't imagine why anyone would want to spend time there.

"Help you?" the bartender asked.

"Just a cola for me," I said.

Harley ordered a beer and asked for a menu. "I heard the burgers in this place are pretty good from my friend, Tim Maverick. You know him?"

"Yeah, I knew him," the bartender answered. "If you're his friend, I guess you know he passed away."

Harley lowered his head. "Yes. I have to say, I was surprised to hear he'd OD'd. He seemed to have gotten his life together. I thought he was doing better."

"Tim was doing fine. He'd come in, sip a cola, and play pool with the guys, but I hadn't seen him take a drink in at least five years."

"What do you think happened that he ended up overdosing on heroin?" Harley asked.

"Between you and me," the bartender leaned in close, even though the three of us were the only ones in the bar, "I don't think he OD'd by accident. I think someone shot him up and left him to die."

"Any idea who might have done such a thing?" Harley asked.

The bartender hesitated before answering. I could see he was weighing his options. "You didn't hear this from me," he said at last. "But Tim found out something damaging about a local dealer. He never did say what he knew, but I heard him talking to some of the guys about not buying from that particular source. The guy was operating in such a way as to attract the attention of the state authorities, so Tim was warning them that if they weren't careful, they might get caught in the crossfire."

"Do you know who Tim was referring to?" I asked.

"He didn't say, but I know the guys usually buy from a guy named Doc. I imagine that's a nickname."

"All drug dealing is illegal," I pointed out. "Do you know why this specific dealer was gaining state attention?"

The bartender shook his head. "Can't say I do. But the men Tim was talking to were current users, and I know they buy quality stuff."

"Quality stuff?" I raised an eyebrow.

"Professional-grade pharmaceuticals, not the homemade stuff."

"Would you be willing to give us the names of the men Tim was warning?" Harley asked.

"No, I couldn't do that. But I'd be okay with mentioning you're interested in speaking with them if they're willing. They may require an incentive, but I think you can get one or two to talk."

Harley jotted down his cell number. "Call me if you get someone who'll speak to me."

"Will do, and don't forget to bring your cash."

We left without finishing our drinks. Gremlins wasn't at all the sort of place I wanted to spend any more time in than I absolutely had to.

"So, what do you think?" I asked after taking several deep gulps of fresh air after the stale air in the dark building.

"I think Shredder and Landon might have been on to something when they suggested there may be more than one motive to explore. If there's a drug dealer in town under investigation and Tim knew something that could lead to his arrest and conviction, I could see that leading to murder. And the fact that Tim was shot up with heroin would fit in that instance."

"What about Tim's cabin being trashed?"

Harley opened my door for me and I slid into the Jeep while he went around to the passenger side.

"I suppose the dealer could have been looking for whatever proof Tim might have had, but there's still the possibility that the person who tossed Tim's cabin isn't the same one who killed him."

"Seems unlikely, but I guess it's possible. We should come up with some sort of a game plan. At this point the only thing that comes to mind is that we try to talk to the people who knew Tim best. We only asked a few questions about his new job when we spoke to them before."

"That might be a good idea. Let's stop by Neverland for lunch and discuss our options."

******

Unlike Gremlins, Neverland smelled heavenly when we entered. The bar was one of my favorite places. Not only was it quaint and cozy, but the food was to die for. But the real draw for me was that anytime I showed up, I found people inside who were happy to see me.

"What's that I smell?" I asked Sarge, who was sitting at the bar, talking to Jake.

"Seafood chowder. I'm making a pot for the dinner crowd."

"It smells fantastic. I'll have to come back for it. In the meantime, can I get one of your famous ham sandwiches?"

"Coming right up."

Harley ordered a sandwich as well, and then we sat down at the bar to chat with Jake.

"What are you two up to today?" he asked as he poured a beer for Harley and a cola for me.

"Harley's buying a house," I offered.

"You don't say. That's great. Are you moving back?"

"At this point, my plan is to spend my off time here," Harley explained. "I'll keep my home in LA as well because there are times I'll need to be there even when I'm not filming."

"We'll be real happy to have you back in Rescue," Jake said. "I went by the shelter yesterday, and I have to say, the group of folks who have been working on the remodel have done a fantastic job. Harm thinks they can get the place open before the spring thaw."

I nodded.

"Any news on Tim's death?" Jake asked just as Sarge emerged from the kitchen with our lunch.

I explained our idea of looking at Tim's death as resulting from something other than his courier job, and our reason for changing our focus.

"That does make a lot of sense," Jake agreed. "Killing a rehabilitated drug addict with an overdose of drugs does sound as if the killer had a personal vendetta against Tim. Either that or it was someone who knew Tim and hoped everyone would think the overdose was an accident."

I took a bite of my sandwich, chewed, and swallowed as I tried to focus my mind on the task before us. Our first stop should probably be either Jared Martin, Teresa Toller, or Pastor Brown, I thought. All would most likely be found at their places of business today.

"Have you ever heard of a drug dealer called Doc?" I asked Jake.

He shook his head. "Doesn't ring a bell. There was a guy in town over the summer who went by the name of Duck, but I heard he was arrested when the cops found the meth lab he'd been operating."

"According to the bartender at Gremlins, which is where Tim used to hang out, this Doc deals in prescription-grade pharmaceuticals."

"Maybe Doc is a real doctor," Jake suggested.

Or a pharmacist, I realized. Could Jared Martin be Doc? No. I rejected that idea before I even had a chance to voice it. Not only were Jared and Tim friends, but Jared seemed to be a legitimate businessman who had an excellent reputation in town.

"I think we should speak to Teresa after we eat," I suggested. "If she was dating Tim, she must have some idea what was going on in his life that might have gotten him killed other than his job. After that, I'd like to see Pastor Brown. If we don't have any new information after that, we'll try Jared again."

"Sounds like a plan to me," Harley answered.

Teresa worked as a cashier at the local five and dime. I was afraid the place would be packed this close to Christmas with holiday shoppers picking up last-minute gifts and decorations, but as it turned out, there was only one person in line when we arrived. I'd pretty much decided to follow through with the tree idea, so I headed to the seasonal aisle to pick up some lights while Harley got in line. By the time I returned to the front of the store, Harley was chatting with Teresa, who seemed barely able to contain her nervousness. I supposed when a movie star as big as Harley walked into your store, it was normal to feel a bit out of sorts.

"Mr. Medford said you had some additional questions for me about Tim," Teresa said when I joined him at the counter.

"I do. And I want to buy these lights as well."

Teresa looked grateful to have something to do with her hands as she rang me up.

"We hit a bit of a dead end with the theory that Tim may have been killed because of something relating to his job, so we're looking at other angles," I began. "Can you think of anything else going on in his life that seemed to be causing him stress or was throwing up any red flags as far as you were concerned?"

"We didn't spend as much time together as people seemed to think. Sure, we were friends, and we went out from time to time, but he spent a lot more time with his volunteer work and his friends than he did with me."

"What sort of volunteer work?" I asked.

"He helped out at the church quite a bit. He did odd jobs for Pastor Brown, and I know he helped deliver food and supplies to the needy. He also ran a Narcotics Anonymous group in the church basement on Monday and Thursday evenings. You might want to speak to Pastor Brown. He spent more time with Tim than I did."

"I will. What can you tell me about Tim's friends?"

"He managed to kick his drug habit, but he missed hanging out with his old friends, so he made plans to play pool with them a couple of times a week. I thought hanging out with his drug buddies was a bad idea, but he seemed to handle it okay. I never noticed any signs that he was using again. I think in his own mind, Tim used his time playing pool with the guys to try to save them."

Harley asked a few more questions that didn't really provide us with anything more than we already knew while I paid for my lights. By the time we left the store, it had started to snow. I looked out toward the horizon, where dark clouds were beginning to gather. It looked like we might be in for another storm.

"Should we head over to the church next?" I asked Harley after we settled into my Jeep.

He turned to look at me. "I know this might sound totally off the wall, but there's an idea rolling around in my head that seems ludicrous that I think should be discussed."

"You think Jared Martin might be Doc," I stated.

Harley looked surprised. "Yes. How did you know?"

"I thought the same thing," I admitted. "Jared seems like a really nice guy. I knew he and Tim were friends, and the first time I spoke to him, he didn't say anything that led me to believe he was selling pharmaceuticals on the black market. Still, we know Tim was now an advocate for a drug-free lifestyle, so what if he found out Jared was dealing drugs and threatened to turn him in? Jared would realize he'd not only be arrested but he'd also lose his license, so he panicked and killed Tim."

Harley and I sat in silence as we let the idea sink in. Harley didn't know Jared, so he probably didn't have a strong reason to reject the idea, but I did, and while the theory made a lot of sense, I couldn't quite wrap my head around it.

"So, even if we believe this could be a possibility, what do we do? Do we just show up at the pharmacy and confront him with our suspicions? Or do we call the police and tell them what we think might have happened to Tim?" Harley asked.

"We have no proof Tim was murdered, so I don't think they'll take what we have to say seriously. Maybe if we come up with something that shows our theory is valid, we could convince them to take a second look."

"Should we speak to Jared directly?" I asked.

"If he did kill Tim, that's a really bad idea. We need to dig around a bit more first. Maybe we should take one more look at Tim's place. This time, we'll specifically look for proof Tim knew who Doc was and planned to expose him."

"Fine by me," I agreed. "Should we go by to speak to Pastor Brown?"

"Let's go to Tim's first. We can always run by the church later."

******

We arrived at Tim's cabin—me for my third time—and headed inside. It still didn't look like anyone had been inside to clean up. Once again, I wondered who Tim's next of kin might be. Someone must have inherited the cabin, although I had no idea who that could be. As I had during my previous two visits, I opened drawers and cupboards and looked under furniture for clues to what could have happened to him.

"I wonder why the police are so sure Tim's death was an accidental overdose when someone obviously broke into his home," I said. "You'd think a break-in coinciding with a death of any sort would send up all sorts of red flags."

Harley picked up a box, looked inside, and put it aside. "That's a good point. Maybe the investigating officer had a specific reason to assume Tim's death was nothing more than an accidental overdose."

"Like what?"

He paused and looked in my direction. "Off the top of my head, we're assuming Tim didn't buy the heroin, but we don't know that for certain. Maybe the police have proof he did. We're also assuming Tim was alone when he died, or at least alone with his killer. What if he wasn't? What if there was a witness we don't know about?" Harley took a deep breath and turned back to the stack of boxes he'd been looking through. "To be honest, if the man in the photo didn't kill Tim, which seems to be the current theory, maybe he really did just fall off the wagon and OD."

I picked up a book and flipped through the pages. "Do you really think that could be what happened?"

He sighed. "I don't know. Maybe. I haven't been close to Tim in a long time. If I'd just heard he OD'd and he hadn't sent me that letter, I would have assumed he'd fallen off the wagon. I know a lot of people who deal with drug and alcohol problems, and it happens. Even after years of sobriety."

I turned in a circle and looked around the room. "I guess the question is, how can we know?"

"Unless we find something conclusive, I'm not sure we can."

"If Tim was in crisis before his death, he would most likely have spoken to his pastor. Let's head over to the church to see if he's willing and able to tell us anything," I said. "We can always come back here if we feel the need."

I had just put my key in the ignition of the Jeep when my phone buzzed. I looked at the caller ID; it was blocked.

"Hello?" I answered.

"Hello, love. Have you missed me?" Shredder asked.

I smiled. "Surprisingly, I have. Is finding out the answer to that question the only reason you called?"

"Actually, no. I wanted to let you know that, thanks to your help and the brave actions of your friend Tim, we now have Pickard in custody."

"That's wonderful."

"The world is a safer place with him out of circulation. He gave us the name of the man who was to buy the thumb drive and we have people on the way to arrest him as well."

"Sounds like you managed to tie everything up nice and neat. Congratulations."

"Just doing my job. I can't talk long; I just wanted you to know how things turned out."

"Before you hang up, did you happen to ask Pickard about Tim?"

"He said he didn't kill him and didn't have him killed. He was angry when Tim didn't make the handoff and he did send someone to his house to look for the thumb drive, but by the time his man arrived in town, Tim was already dead. I need to hang up, but thanks again for everything."

The line went dead.

I looked at Harley, who was watching me with a curious expression on his face.

"That was Shredder. He wanted to let me know he caught up with Pickard. The man is in custody and will most likely never see the light of day again."

"That's great. Did your friend ask Pickard whether he killed Tim?"

"Shredder said he didn't do it. Pickard sent someone to recover the drive, but Tim was already dead when he got there."

"Which could mean the police don't even know the house has been tossed," Harley pointed out.

"Okay, how's this for a theory," I began. "Bear with me while I restate some of what we already know. Tim stopped at the gas station on his way north. We can assume he had the thumb drive with him, and that he decided at some point not to hand it off as he was supposed to. He stopped at the bar and hid it in the bathroom. He then came back to Rescue;

we can assume he went to his home because we found the gas receipt from his fill-up on his way out of town there. Somehow, he OD'd the next night. The police discovered his body shortly after he died. They could very well have come by his home to check things out, but they didn't find anything out of order. Tim had a history with drugs, so when his body was found, they assumed he fell off the wagon and OD'd. Meanwhile, Pickard found out the drop didn't happen. He probably tried to get hold of Tim, who was already dead and so not returning his calls. He sent a thug to try to locate the drive, which was the point at which the cabin was trashed. It seems reasonable no one knew about that until you and I and Jake stopped by on that first day."

I looked at Harley, who had a contemplative look on his face.

"That all makes sense," Harley admitted. "But why did he OD?"

I paused before I answered. "Everyone we've spoken to has said Tim was clean in the days before his death, but they've also said he was worried and stressed out. Tim was so worried, in fact, that he sent you the note and the photo of Pickard. I suppose that amount of stress, coupled with his decision not to turn over the thumb drive, could have led him to seek comfort in numbness. He must have known Pickard would come after him."

Harley didn't answer right away, but I knew he was considering the situation. "I can buy your theory up to a point. The thing is, why would Tim buy heroin when his drugs of choice were cocaine and painkillers when he was using? And why shoot up in a ditch? Why not come back to his cabin and get high in the comfort of his own home?"

"I suppose he might have fled when he realized Pickard would be looking for him. Maybe the place he died is where he met the dealer."

Harley tilted his head. "I suppose it could have gone down that way. But again, why heroin? The stuff is nasty. The possibility of overdose is pretty high compared to other drugs he might have found relief from his stress with."

I cringed as I had a horrible thought. "What if that was the reason he chose heroin?"

Harley frowned. "Are you suggesting he committed suicide?"

"Maybe. He had to know that by hiding the thumb drive and failing to make the exchange, Pickard would hunt him down and kill him, although he might very well have tortured him first. Maybe he decided to take matters into his own hands." I hated that this theory made sense, but I could see that might very well have been how things had played out. I felt certain that when Tim took the courier job he didn't realize he was transporting sensitive information, but it seemed he figured it out at some point. Maybe he wanted out, but Pickard wouldn't let him go. He might even have threatened the lives of those close to Tim. Maybe Tim intended to make that last drop, but his conscious got the better of him, so he hid the drive, came home, and ended his life before Pickard got to him.

"How can we know?" Harley asked.

"We need to talk to Pastor Brown. If Tim intended to end his life, he might have taken the opportunity to clear his conscious first."

When we arrived at the church, the pastor said he couldn't betray any confidences Tim might have shared, but I explained our theory, then asked him if he thought it held any water. He admitted it was a very good theory indeed.

After we left the church, Harley and I headed to my place. I needed to feed the puppies and let the dogs out.

"So, is that it?" Harley asked as we walked through the woods with the dogs.

"I suppose that's up to you. But if Tim used the heroin of his own volition, whether he intended to kill himself or not, I'm not sure there's much more we can do."

"It seems wrong somehow to stop looking before we know for sure."

We walked in silence, each in our own thoughts. I felt our new theory made more sense than any of the others, but I also wondered why, if Tim had realized his days were numbered and decided to take control of his own death, he'd chosen drugs as his method of suicide. He'd been an advocate for a drug-free lifestyle for a while. The use of drugs as his last statement in this life just didn't fit, and that's what I said to Harley after a bit.

"I agree."

"So, we keep looking?"

Harley nodded. "I say we stay the course until we know for sure one way or the other."

Chapter 16

Harley left after we walked the dogs because I had to get ready for the cookie exchange that evening. I wasn't in the mood to go, but I'd promised Chloe and, for some reason, it was important to her. I showered and changed, took one last look around, then headed out. It appeared the bad weather I'd noticed earlier in the day was still lurking on the horizon.

I drove down Main on my way to Chloe's Café, where the exchange was being held. As I passed the pharmacy, I saw Jared's car in the alley. Despite everything we'd learned, the idea that Jared was Doc had been lingering in the back of my mind. I pulled into the lot and parked. I probably shouldn't just walk in and say, "Hey, Jared, how's it going? Say, you aren't running a drug business on the side using the alias Doc, are you?"

Even though I didn't have a plan, I found myself getting out of the Jeep and walking up to the front door of the pharmacy. Unfortunately, it was locked. I could see a light on in the back, so I decided, probably unwisely, to go around to the door there in the hope it would be unlocked.

It was.

I could hear voices coming from Jared's office, so I slowly crept into the storage area and listened.

"I told you the price for this product was going up the last time you were here," a voice that sounded like Jared's said.

"I know you did, but I'm not made of money," another man, whose voice I didn't recognize, answered.

"The price stands. Do you want it or not?"

"Yeah, I want it, but I'm not happy about the price change," the second man complained.

It sounded like a drug deal could be going on, but it also could be a legit pharmacy customer who had come by after hours and wasn't happy that the cost for his prescription had changed. I needed to get closer, so I slowly scooted toward the office door.

"Did Frank come by?" the voice that didn't belong to Jared asked.

"Not yet. He knows I need to leave by eight. Will you want the same order next week?"

"Yeah," the second man groaned. "Not like I can take my business elsewhere."

I plastered my body against the wall when I realized the men were leaving the office. I hoped they wouldn't notice me in the dim light.

They did.

"Harmony, what are you doing here?" Jared asked.

I tried not to look as terrified as I suddenly felt. "I saw your car in the alley and wanted to talk to you some more about Tim."

"Isn't that the dude you had me off?" the second man blurted out.

"You killed him?" I asked, totally stunned. Even though the reason I'd stopped there tonight was because I suspected Jared could be guilty, I was still surprised to have that suspicion confirmed.

"Nice going, Bruno," Jared said with a look of irritation on his face.

"Hey, the broad heard us talking. I knew you were going to have to eliminate her anyway, so what's the big deal?"

"You're going to kill me?" I screeched.

I glanced at Jared, who looked conflicted. I hoped he would have enough of a conscious to cut me some slack and let me go.

He didn't. "Take her to the icehouse."

The icehouse? I knew there was an abandoned building just outside of town that had been used as an icehouse at some point. In fact, if I remembered correctly, it was very close to where Tim's body had been found.

"You aren't planning to shoot me up with heroin, are you?" I asked as Bruno dragged me to his truck.

"No reason to. No one would believe you fell off the wagon. Someone would, however, believe you went out on a rescue and froze to death."

I tried to wrap my head around exactly what was going to happen as Bruno tossed me into his truck, then took off from the alley with tires peeling. I knew I had to get out of the truck and I had to do it fast, but I had no idea how I was going to escape a man who weighed at least twice what I did *and* had a gun.

When we arrived at the icehouse, I tried to make a run for it, but he grabbed me by the arm so hard, I knew he'd left a bruise, then dragged me into the dark building. I couldn't see much, just enough to know he was headed to the insulation room where the ice was stored years ago. I knew I should scream, but I couldn't catch my breath as Bruno opened the door and tossed me inside. My heart fell to my feet when I heard him lock the door from the outside. The idiot planned to leave me here to suffocate.

I needed to do something—anything—but I was frozen with fear. I'm not sure how long I just stood there in the dark before my mind began to work again. The room was totally dark, but I had my phone. It provided light but, unfortunately, there wasn't any service in the enclosed room.

I tried the door, but it was locked, as I'd thought. I looked around but didn't see another point of exit. I knew the room must be airtight, but it was large, so I wouldn't run out of air right away.

I needed to think. I needed Jake.

I sat down on the floor near the door and focused my energy. I'd only recently been able to intentionally connect with those I chose, and only within a rescue. I'd never connected with someone who wasn't in need of rescue, and the only two-way communication that had been successful had been with the little girl in the car accident. Still, I had to try. It seemed to be the only card in my deck.

I calmed my nerves, took a deep breath, and closed my eyes. I focused all my energy on Jake's face. I knew he was at Neverland, so I focused on that as well.

Jake. I need you. Please hear me.

I waited, but he wasn't coming through.

Jake. Please listen. I need to be rescued.

I still wasn't seeing anything, but I had to keep trying and pushed every other thought from my mind. It took me about ten minutes, but I finally was able to make a one-way connection. I could see Jake. He was standing at the bar, talking to Wyatt.

Jake. Please listen. I need you.

I could see Jake turn his head slightly, as if he may have heard me on some level and was looking for the source of the voice.

Jake. It's Harmony. Please listen.

"Harmony?" Jake said out loud.

"She's not here," Wyatt responded with an odd look on his face. "Cookie exchange, remember."

Jake rubbed his forehead, then returned his attention to Wyatt.

Jake, it's Harmony. I'm in trouble. I need you.

Jake looked startled, a frown on his face. "I think Harmony is trying to make a connection with me."

"Can she do that?" Wyatt asked.

"Her powers are growing. She made a two-way connection with a child a few days ago. She walked her through the steps she needed to save the life of her whole family."

"If Harmony can speak to you, you best listen," Wyatt said. "Sit down here at this table. Close your eyes and focus on her face."

Thank you, Wyatt.

Once Jake was seated, I tried again.

Jake, it's Harmony. I'm in trouble.

"I'm here for you, babe," Jake said aloud. "Where are you?"

The icehouse on the north edge of town. I'm locked in the freezer. Jared killed Tim and now he's trying to kill me.

Jake opened his eyes. He looked at Wyatt. "Harm is locked in the freezer of the icehouse north of town. Grab the gear; we need to go."

I took a deep breath and let the connection fade. I felt totally drained, as if someone had opened me up and siphoned out every ounce of energy I possessed. Now that Jake was on his way, I let the terror I felt penetrate my consciousness. By the time Jake and Wyatt found me, I was in the fetal position, sobbing uncontrollably.

******

"Better?" Jake asked as he handed me my second glass of brandy. I was curled up on my sofa, clinging to Moose like a lifeline.

"I'll be okay. I'm just tired. So tired."

Jake sat down on the sofa. He took his hand in mine. He used one finger to tilt my chin so he was looking me in the eye. "Do you realize what just happened?"

"You rescued me. You always do."

"It's not that. We connected. You were in trouble and you managed to make your voice heard in my mind."

I smiled. "It was pretty awesome. Exhausting, but awesome."

"Do you think you can do that whenever you want? Communicate telepathically?"

I shook my head. "I don't think so. In the past, I've only been able to connect when someone has needed to be rescued. Today, it was me in need of rescue. I have a feeling the link is the rescue situation. Or maybe it has to do with extreme fear. Or emotion.

I don't think I can just hop into the mind of anyone I choose."

"Maybe not, but it was still amazing."

I hugged Jake. "When I realized I was going to suffocate, I knew I had to try, but I also knew my odds of success were slim. I realized I needed to choose very carefully and I knew that of all the people in my life, you would be the most likely to accept my voice in your head and go with it."

Jake hugged me so tightly, I thought he might break a rib.

"I'm okay," I assured him. "We're okay."

Jake pulled back and kissed me on the forehead. "You look exhausted. You should get some rest."

"I don't want to be alone."

"I'll stay. Go get ready for bed. I'll see to the animals."

I was just drifting off to sleep when I felt the weight of Jake's body on the bed beside me. I entwined my fingers with his as I drifted off to sleep, depleted but somehow content.

Chapter 17

Sunday, December 24

"You'd better hurry if you don't want to be late," Harley called to me over the Christmas carols playing in the background.

"I'll be right there," I called back as I worked the clasp of the necklace Val had given me for Christmas the year before she died.

We were on our way to the Christmas Eve celebration Jake was hosting at Neverland for the search-and-rescue family. Harley's offer on the house had been accepted, so he'd gone ahead and bought a heavy-duty four-wheel drive he planned to leave in Rescue. He was leaving for a shoot on January 2, so Jake had told him he could leave it at his place until he closed on the house.

I glanced at the small tree in the corner of my room. Harley had helped me cut and decorate it the day after I'd been rescued from the freezer. After I gave my statement to the police, Jared and his partner in crime had been arrested for dealing drugs, as well as attempted murder. They were investigating Tim's death as well, and it seemed only a matter of time before a murder charge was added to the package.

Beneath the tree were two wrapped packages. I'd already loaded the packages for Jake and the gang into Harley's new truck, but I'd kept two back. One was for Harley, and I planned to give it to him tomorrow, when he came over for breakfast, and the other was to me from Shredder. I'd received the gift two days ago but had yet to open it.

"So, what do you think?" I asked Honey, who had moved her puppies onto the bed two days ago. I'd tried several times to return them to the closet, but she kept moving them back to the bed, so I pushed the bed against the wall and set up pillow barriers so they couldn't fall off. "Should we see what Shredder sent?"

Honey barked. I knew she'd adored Shredder and I imagined she hoped he'd come back. I doubted he would, but it was nice of him to send a gift. I crossed the room and picked up the package. I carefully removed the paper to find a framed photo of Santa and me, the one Shredder had taken the night we'd stayed at the inn. I couldn't help but smile.

I glanced at the package I'd wrapped for Harley. "Why is it," I asked Honey, "I've had a rash of unavailable men dropped into my lap?"

I'd been attracted to Harley since the first time I'd seen him in the hall of the high school. He'd been a sophomore and I'd been a freshman, and I'd vowed at that moment that he would be mine. Of course, the life I'd imagined for us together hadn't been destined to be, but we'd always have the kiss, and if he came to town from time to time, we could have a friendship as well.

I ran my finger around the frame. I didn't really know the man who'd dropped into my life only to disappear in a flash, but we'd shared something while he was here, and despite my desire not to do so, I'd miss him.

"I might be late," I said to Honey. "Your babies have been fed, so you should be in good shape until I do get home. I'll leave the lamp on if you'd like."

Honey thumped her tail against the mattress as I walked out of the bedroom.

"Ready," I said to Harley as I walked into the living room, where he'd been waiting.

"You look beautiful. I love the red sweater. Very festive."

"I'm usually more of a black and brown sort of girl, but it's Christmas. Who am I to ignore tradition?"

"I'm glad you said that," Harley said as he reached into his jacket pocket and pulled out a sprig of mistletoe. He lifted it into the air, took a step forward, and proceeded to give me the second-best kiss I'd ever received in my life. Who would have thought the second-best kiss would come from the same dark-haired boy who'd delivered the best kiss on the high school stage all those years ago?

Up Next From Kathi Daley Books

Preview *The Cat of Christmas Future*

Chapter 1

Wednesday, December 13

There was, admittedly, more popcorn on the floor than on the tree, but I still considered our night's endeavor to be a success. The annual production of the Christmas story, performed by the children's choir at St. Patrick's Catholic Church, was just nine days away and my fiancé, Cody West, and I were supervising the children who would portray the characters as they decorated the church auditorium in preparation for the throngs of proud parents and grandparents who planned to attend. I'd always loved this season, but it seemed even more special this year as Cody and I discussed traditions and planned our life together.

"Everything looks just perfect," Father Bartholomew complimented us as he walked up behind me.

"Thank you," I said as the song playing in the background changed from "Silent Night" to "The First Noel." "I think it's coming together nicely."

"I especially love the lights around all the windows. They give the whole room a festive feel."

"The kids wanted to go all out because this will be your first Christmas with us." Father Bartholomew was a young priest who had come to St. Patrick's earlier in the year after our longtime priest, Father Kilian, retired.

"I appreciate how welcome everyone has made me feel. I'll admit to being somewhat nervous about trying to fill Father Kilian's shoes. I'm fairly new at this and Father Kilian has been such an important fixture in the community for so many years."

"He has," I agreed. "And he'll continue to be a member of the community even in retirement, but we're very happy to have you with us. In fact, I'd like to invite you to the annual Christmas Eve dinner Cody and I prepare for those who may not have other plans over the holiday. It's held at the home of Mr. Parsons, the man Cody lives with and looks out for."

"Why, thank you. I'd enjoy that very much."

"Great," I answered as I placed my hand on the shoulder of one of the boys as he ran past us, tailing a chain of red and green construction paper. I raised an eyebrow at Robby, who took my silent hint to slow down and did so. "I'll get you the address. If you come across any other parishioners who are going to be alone for the holiday, feel free to bring them along. Cody and I want to be sure everyone has somewhere to go."

"Thank you again. That's very kind of you. It warms my heart the way this congregation welcomes newcomers. In fact, there's a newcomer I'd like you to meet." Father Bartholomew waved to a man who had just entered the room. He walked toward us, and the two men shook hands. "Caitlin Hart, I'd like you to meet Richard Sinclair. As I indicated, Richard is new to the island and to St. Pat's."

"I'm happy to meet you, Richard." I shook his hand.

"Please call me Rich."

"Okay, then, nice to meet you, Rich. Most people call me Cait."

"I'm hoping to talk Mr. Sinclair into filling the vacancy we have with the adult choir. He was a member of the choir at the church he previously attended, and I think he'll do quite well in the role of director."

"We could use the help," I seconded.

The tall, dark-haired man with silver streaks paused before he answered. "I told Father Bartholomew I'd consider it, but I have a lot on my plate right now. Still, I'd like to see the facility."

"I have a church council to get to," Father Bartholomew said, "but perhaps Cait could walk you over to the choir room and show you around."

I smiled. "Sure. I'd be happy to. Just let me tell Cody what I'm doing."

I wiped a streak of glitter from my cheek and filled Cody in on my errand, then returned to Rich, motioning for him to follow me. "So, how long have you lived on the island?" I asked conversationally.

"Just a few weeks. I purchased the abandoned warehouse on the east side of the island. I'm planning to renovate it and turn it into a high-end restaurant."

"That's a wonderful location for a restaurant, but I have a feeling you'd be better off tearing the whole thing down and starting over. It's in pretty bad shape."

"Perhaps. My contractor will be here on Monday and we'll have that conversation. If I do tear it down I'd want to repurpose some of the wood. It's aged and rustic, exactly the sort of thing I'm going for."

"What sort of a restaurant are you planning to open?" I asked as we headed across the property toward the main building.

"An upscale Italian restaurant with an extensive steak-house menu as well. I worked in a similar place when I lived in Seattle and it did quite well."

I paused. "A high-end restaurant might work in Seattle, but Madrona Island is pretty casual. You might want to consider offering some items geared toward our working-class lifestyle. I'm sure you'd attract visitors to the island with a high-end menu, but honestly, I don't think you'd get much business from the locals. Tourism on the island dries up in the winter, so unless you only plan to be open seasonally, you'll need business from the island's residents as well as tourists."

"Thank you for the input. I'll take your comments into consideration when I make up my final menu."

Once we entered the main parish structure, I opened the door to the music room and stepped inside. "Here we are. It's small, but it's home."

"It's nice; I like it," Rich said, entering the room behind me. He took several steps inside, looking around as he went.

"Cody and I practice on Wednesdays and the children's choir services the eleven o'clock Mass on Sundays. Currently the adult choir practices on both Tuesdays and Thursdays and performs during both the eight o'clock service on Sunday and the seven-thirty service on Saturday night. If you agree to take over you can discuss the specifics with Father Bartholomew."

"Thank you. I'll definitely think over his offer. I enjoy being part of a choir, but I'm not sure I have time to take the lead. I'll have a lot to do if I want to get the restaurant open by spring, starting with the eviction of the squatters who're living there right now."

I frowned. "There are people living there?"

"Not legally, but the place has been empty for so long that a group of homeless people have set up camp. The first thing I need to do before I can start on the renovation is to convince the resident deputy to kick everyone out."

My heart filled with sympathy for those individuals who would be displaced. "It's Christmas. Can't the eviction wait until after the first of the year?"

"Not if I want to meet my opening deadline." Rich looked around the room. "I know you need to get back to the kids. Would you mind if I stay and poke around a bit?"

"Not at all. I'll be in the auditorium if you need anything."

As I walked back to where Cody and the kids were waiting, a feeling of déjà vu washed over me. Two years ago Cody and I had been helping the choir kids to decorate on a Wednesday evening when a beautiful cat named Ebenezer showed up. Like tonight, it had been snowing, and like tonight, I'd found out that a local business owner planned to put people out on the street just days before Christmas. Cody and I had been able to stop it then and I wondered if we weren't meant to intervene now. Of course this situation was different. The tenants living in Balthazar Pottage's apartment building had been living there legally and, I felt, had the right to be given additional notice if they had to move. Additionally, Balthazar was a reclusive miser who could well afford to wait a few days to give the tenants time to make other arrangements. I wasn't sure whether Rich Sinclair had the financial means to put off the renovation of the warehouse and I wasn't sure exactly what I could do to stop Rich from evicting squatters, but I intended to find out exactly who was living in the building. Hopefully, Cody and I could come up with a plan to help them relocate.

"The place looks great," I said when I returned to the auditorium, where red and green lights strung from the ceiling twinkled to the sound of the carols playing in the background. "Very festive."

"I think the kids did a good job. Did you get the new choir director settled?"

"I showed him the room, but I'm less than convinced he's actually going to take on the duties associated with running the choir. He just moved to the island and it sounds like he already has a lot of things to do."

"It's hard to find volunteers who have the time to take on the larger roles."

"Yes, I guess it is. The choir commitment takes a lot of our time, but I wouldn't give it up for anything."

"I agree." Cody smiled. "Speaking of a time commitment, while you were gone the kids asked if we were going to meet more than once next week."

"I think we should. The play is on Saturday, so let's have the kids meet in the choir room on Monday and Wednesday, and then we'll have a dress rehearsal on Friday. I'll go over to Father Bartholomew's office to run off flyers with the dates and times. It would probably be best if we sent the information home tonight."

"Okay. I'll have everyone start cleaning up."

I was halfway back to the main church building where the offices and choir room were located when a cat I knew well ran across the lawn toward me. "Ebenezer, what are you doing here?"

"Meow."

The feeling of déjà vu I'd had minutes before suddenly intensified. I'd first met him on that snowy Wednesday two years ago. Looking back, I knew he'd come to help me with the huge task I'd taken on. I had to wonder if he wasn't here again for a similar purpose.

"It's coming down pretty hard; let's get inside." I picked up the large, furry cat and continued toward the office, where the copier was kept. I should probably try to contact Balthazar to let him know I had his cat. Ebenezer seemed to come and go as he pleased, but I knew the old man was firmly attached to him and thought he might worry if he was gone too long without a word,

I set Ebenezer on the floor while I grabbed a Sharpie and penned a note with the dates and times of practice the following week. Then I placed the paper on the copier and pressed the button to make thirty copies, which would be more than enough. I was waiting for the ancient machine to crank them out when I heard a voice raised in anger. The voice sounded like Rich's and seemed to be coming from down the hall. I supposed he could still be in the choir room but who was in there with him? Whatever was going on was none of my business and I probably shouldn't listen, but I couldn't seem to quell my natural curiosity and found myself inching toward the partially open door.

"I don't care what you have to do to get them out, just do it."

The voice, which I confirmed did belong to Rich, paused. When I didn't hear a response I assumed he was on the phone.

"Yes, even the girl. I know her situation, but the fact that she's homeless and pregnant isn't my problem. I have a contractor coming to the island on Monday. If the place isn't empty by then heads are going to roll."

Yikes. The situation sounded worse than I'd thought. Monday was just five days away, not a lot of time to relocate a bunch of people. I grabbed the stack of copies I'd made and headed back to the auditorium. Once the kids had been picked up I'd share what I knew with Cody. Maybe between the two of us we could come up with at least a temporary solution.

"I have the rehearsal schedule," I held up the flyers.

"Great." Cody took them from me. He turned and looked at the kids, who had gathered their possessions in preparation for pickup. "I have flyers I need each of you to give to a parent. We'll be having extra rehearsals next week as we prepare for our performance and I need everyone to attend every rehearsal."

The kids, who were thrilled to see Ebenezer had come for a visit, played with the cat and chatted among themselves as Cody passed out the flyers. Parents had begun to arrive and I wanted to be sure all of them had the information, so I stood at the door to catch anyone who might not have received one.

"I have a rehearsal schedule for next week," I said to one of the moms, whose son was messing around and hadn't taken a flyer.

"Great." She smiled. "I was wondering if you were going to have extra rehearsals. I hear congratulations are in order. Have you set the date?"

"Thank you and not yet. Cody and I decided to wait until after the first of the year to discuss specifics. There's so much going on right now, everything seems a bit overwhelming."

She placed her hand on my arm. "I don't blame you for taking your time. When I got engaged I was so excited I bought a dress the very next day. Over the course of the nine months I planned a huge wedding and was stressed the entire time. If I had it to do over again I'd take my time and plan something special to us, not just something big and flashy."

"We feel the same way. We have a lot of family and friends, so I'm not sure small will work, but I'm definitely thinking simple."

"It sounds like you have the beginnings of a plan." The woman looked around the room, located her son, and waved him over. "We should get going. Congratulations again."

I thanked her and moved on to the next parent who seemed to be lacking a flyer. Once the kids had all been delivered to their parents, Cody and I cleaned up and headed, along with Ebenezer, toward my cabin. I filled him in on what I knew of the warehouse situation as we drove.

Cody being the smart and wonderful man he is jumped right in with an idea. "I think the first thing we need to do is find out exactly who's living in the building and what their situation is. There may be people who have a place to go if provided with the means to get there, and others who have a long-term plan and only require short-term housing. I think I can work out a deal with the motor lodge for short-term housing if needed. We'll drive out there first thing in the morning and figure out what's what."

"Okay, that sounds great." I glanced at Ebenezer, who was sitting on the seat between us. "I should go talk to Balthazar as well. He owns several apartment buildings. Maybe he'd be willing to help out if he has vacancies."

"We can see him tomorrow after we visit the warehouse."

"Don't you have that guy coming from the ad agency tomorrow?" I asked.

Cody grimaced. "I do; I almost forgot. He isn't coming until eleven, though, so we can still visit the warehouse in the morning. We can see Balthazar the following day, or you can catch the morning ferry and go on your own tomorrow."

"I'll go alone. Ebenezer can come with me. If Mr. Sinclair is serious about having everyone out by Monday we don't have time to waste."

"You should let Finn know what's going on too," Cody said, referring to my brother-in-law, who happened to be the island's resident deputy. "If Sinclair plans to use force to get the squatters out Finn can ensure that things are handled legally and without violence."

"Good idea. I'll call him when we get to my cabin." I glanced out the window at the still-falling snow. "I know we talked about going out for dinner on the way home, but I think we should head back before the roads get bad. I've got some soup left over from last night and another loaf of bread in the freezer."

"Sounds good. I want to pop in to check on Mr. Parsons. I'll drop you and Ebenezer off at your place, check on him, and then meet you at the cabin."

It did my heart good to see how much Cody cared for the elderly man he shared a space with. There'd been a time when Mr. Parsons was a bit of a grump, but ever since Cody had remodeled and moved into the third floor of his huge oceanfront mansion, Mr. Parsons had let go of his anxiety, and almost everyone agreed he was a changed man.

After Cody dropped Ebenezer and me off I took my dog Max out for a quick run, then got our houseguest set up with kitty food and a cat box. When both animals were fed and settled I called Finn. He didn't answer his cell, so I tried the house.

"Oh, hey, Siobhan," I greeted my sister when she answered the phone. "I'm looking for Finn, but he didn't answer his cell."

"He's out on a call. There's a pretty bad accident along the west shore."

"Oh no. I'm so sorry to hear that. Were there injuries?"

"I don't know," Siobhan said. "I haven't heard. I hope not."

"Yeah, me too. I love the snow, but there's always an increase in auto accidents when the roads are icy."

"People don't want to slow down."

"So, how's the packing going?" I asked. Finn and Siobhan had sold Finn's house and bought a larger one together.

"It's been hectic. This place closes in just a few days and we need to be completely moved out by the end of the weekend."

"Don't overdo," I warned my pregnant sister.

"I'm trying not to, but everything is going so fast. It's a bit overwhelming, and to make matters worse, there seems to be a problem with the house we're buying."

I frowned. "Problem? What sort of problem?"

"It seems the woman who's selling it is getting cold feet. To be honest, I've been wondering if that house was the right one for us anyway. It only has three bedrooms, and Finn thinks we should have four. Part of me hopes the sale falls through so we can look for a larger place, but part of me is panicked because we have to be out of here and will have to figure out somewhere to go until we find something else."

"Can you put off the people moving into this house?"

"Not really," Siobhan answered. "The couple is moving here from the East Coast. I'd hate to mess them up. We're thinking about just putting our stuff into storage and seeing if we can stay with Maggie for a while."

Our Aunt Maggie lived in the main house on the property where I had my little cabin on the beach. "I'm sure she'd love to have you. Mom and Cassie are there while the condo is being worked on and Danny is there for the winter, but Maggie has a ton of guest rooms."

"She's always said we're welcome to stay there whenever we need to. I need to get back to packing, but I can pass a message on to Finn when he gets back if you want to fill me in."

I explained to Siobhan, who also happened to be the mayor of Madrona Island, that there was a new man in town intent on kicking a group of homeless people out onto the street with almost no notice. She of course was appalled, especially when she heard one of the squatters might be pregnant. Being pregnant herself, she was extra sensitive to the needs of women in the same condition.

"I understand he needs to have the building vacated to renovate. And I understand it's his building and he has the right to expect he can do with it as he pleases. But to kick a bunch of people out into the snow so close to Christmas seems heartless."

"I agree," I said. "I overheard him on the phone and it sounded like he was willing to resort to any means necessary to get the people out. I don't know for a fact that he'd use violence, but that was the vibe I was picking up. Cody and I are going over to the warehouse tomorrow morning to see exactly what the situation is and how many people will be displaced."

"That sounds like a good idea. I'll fill Finn in when he gets home. I'm not saying squatters don't need to be moved, but let's see if we can find them an alternative place to wait out the winter."

I hung up with Siobhan and tossed a log on the fire, then put the soup in a pan to heat. I defrosted the bread in the microwave and popped it into the oven to brown. The lights on the tree Cody and I had decorated reflected off the snowy window, giving the entire cabin a warm, cozy feeling. I'd just turned on some carols when Cody pulled into the drive. I hoped he'd be able to stay over tonight, but he didn't like to leave Mr. Parsons alone more often than he needed to. At some point we were going to have to discuss living arrangements after we married, but for now we were taking it slow and letting things develop naturally.

"Is Mr. Parsons okay?" I asked as Cody entered through the side door.

"He's watching old movies with Francine." Francine Rivers owned a third of the peninsula where Cody and I resided. When the founding fathers of the island divided it up, one section went to Francine's family, one to Mr. Parsons's, and last to the Harts. Aunt Maggie lived in the big house on the property, and I lived in the summer cabin, which was right on the water and perfect for just me. Once Cody and I were married I'd probably need to move into Mr. Parsons's house with him.

"Can you stay over?" I asked.

Cody nodded. "I'll check on Mr. Parsons in the morning before we head over to the warehouse. Did you get hold of Finn?"

"He's out on a call, but I spoke to Siobhan and she'll fill him in when he gets home."

"Great. Let's eat. I'm starving."

We settled in with our soup and hot bread in front of the crackling fire. We didn't get a lot of snow on Madrona Island, but every year I found myself wishing for Christmas snow. We'd been lucky and had had December snow several years in a row. It really added to the Christmassy feel I'd learned to embrace when I was a child.

"Did you ever find out what was going on with your mom's condo?" Cody asked.

"She said the pipes are shot and they need to completely replumb the whole place. She has to be out for a month, so she and Cassie have moved in with Maggie for the time being."

"Wow, that's tough."

I shrugged. "I guess. I don't think Maggie minds, despite the fact that Danny has moved in for the winter and I now it seems Finn and Siobhan need a place to stay as well."

"I thought they were moving into their new house."

"It looks like it might fall out of escrow and their house is ready to close. It'll be a bit crowded, but Maggie's house is big, and she never minds having the various members of the Hart family staying with her when they need to."

It really did seem the entire Hart clan, other than my oldest brother, Aiden, had lived with Maggie at one time or another. Danny owned a whale-watch boat he lived in, but every now and again he leased it out for the winter and bunked with Maggie to save money during the off season. Siobhan had lived with Maggie after returning to Madrona Island from Seattle, and I'd lived with her in the big house before we renovated the cabin. This was the second time my mom and my youngest sister, Cassie, had stayed with Maggie in recent years, and I imagined it wouldn't be the last. I was just finishing my soup when my phone rang.

It was Siobhan. "Did you talk to Finn?"

"Finn isn't back yet. He's at the hospital."

My heart skipped a beat. "Is he hurt?"

"He's with Aiden. Aiden was involved in the accident Finn responded to."

I put my hand to my mouth, fighting back panic. "Is he—?"

"He's going to be okay. He was driving home from the north shore and hit a patch of ice. His car slid off the road and rolled twice, but the airbag deployed and he was buckled in, so he wasn't seriously injured. Finn said not to come down. They have him sedated and he's resting. Finn's going to get all the details from the doctor and he'll fill us in when he sees us."

"Cody and I will come over to your place."

"No, don't come here, go to Maggie's. Mom, Cassie, and Danny are already there. I'm heading over as well. Finn said he'd meet us there."

When we arrived at Maggie's, the others were all sitting around discussing the situation. "Have you heard anything?" Mom asked as soon as we walked in.

"No. I just spoke to Siobhan and she said to come here. Finn will be joining us as soon as he's able to."

"I know Siobhan said to stay put, but I feel like we should be at the hospital," Danny said.

"There isn't anything we can do. Finn said Aiden is sedated and resting comfortably. With the weather the way it is, waiting really is the best choice."

The room fell silent. I understood that. We didn't know anything, so we couldn't talk about what had happened, and it seemed sort of strange to make chitchat. I hoped Siobhan got here soon. Of all the Harts, she seemed to be the best at knowing exactly what to say. Fortunately, we didn't have long to wait; she arrived shortly after Cody and I did.

"I spoke to Finn again," she began. "Aiden's going to be fine. His car is pretty much totaled, but he managed to come away with nothing more serious than a broken leg and a sprained wrist."

"So nothing life threatening?" Mom asked.

"Nothing life threatening," Siobhan confirmed. "Finn said Aiden will be released tomorrow, as long as he has somewhere to go where he can get help."

"He'll come here," Maggie spoke up. "I have plenty of room, and there will be lots of folks to help out."

"I thought you'd feel that way and so did Finn, so he arranged to have the hospital call him when Aiden's ready to be released. He'll pick him up and bring him here."

I could feel the tension in the room dissipate as everyone began to discuss which room to put Aiden in. We all agreed it should be one of the rooms on the first floor with its own bath. I had a feeling poor Aiden was going to be mothered to death with Mom and Maggie both here, but he'd been on his own for a while now, so perhaps he wouldn't mind.

Books by Kathi Daley

Come for the murder, stay for the romance.

Zoe Donovan Cozy Mystery:

Halloween Hijinks
The Trouble With Turkeys
Christmas Crazy
Cupid's Curse
Big Bunny Bump-off
Beach Blanket Barbie
Maui Madness
Derby Divas
Haunted Hamlet
Turkeys, Tuxes, and Tabbies
Christmas Cozy
Alaskan Alliance
Matrimony Meltdown
Soul Surrender
Heavenly Honeymoon
Hopscotch Homicide
Ghostly Graveyard
Santa Sleuth
Shamrock Shenanigans
Kitten Kaboodle
Costume Catastrophe
Candy Cane Caper
Holiday Hangover
Easter Escapade
Camp Carter
Trick or Treason
Reindeer Roundup – *December 2017*

Zimmerman Academy The New Normal
Ashton Falls Cozy Cookbook

Tj Jensen Paradise Lake Mysteries by Henery Press

Pumpkins in Paradise
Snowmen in Paradise
Bikinis in Paradise
Christmas in Paradise
Puppies in Paradise
Halloween in Paradise
Treasure in Paradise
Fireworks in Paradise
Beaches in Paradise – *June 2018*
Turkeys in Paradise – *November 2018*

Whales and Tails Cozy Mystery:

Romeow and Juliet
The Mad Catter
Grimm's Furry Tail
Much Ado About Felines
Legend of Tabby Hollow
Cat of Christmas Past
A Tale of Two Tabbies
The Great Catsby
Count Catula
The Cat of Christmas Present
A Winter's Tail
The Taming of the Tabby
Frankencat
The Cat of Christmas Future – *November 2017*

Seacliff High Mystery:

The Secret
The Curse
The Relic
The Conspiracy
The Grudge
The Shadow
The Haunting

Sand and Sea Hawaiian Mystery:

Murder at Dolphin Bay
Murder at Sunrise Beach
Murder at the Witching Hour
Murder at Christmas
Murder at Turtle Cove
Murder at Water's Edge
Murder at Midnight

Writers' Retreat Southern Seashore Mystery:

First Case
Second Look
Third Strike
Fourth Victim
Fifth Night – *January 2018*

A Tess and Tilly Cozy Mystery

The Christmas Letter – *December 2017*

Rescue Alaska Paranormal Mystery
Finding Justice
Finding Answers – *2018*

Road to Christmas Romance:
Road to Christmas Past

USA Today best-selling author Kathi Daley lives in beautiful Lake Tahoe with her husband Ken. When she isn't writing, she likes spending time hiking the miles of desolate trails surrounding her home. She has authored more than seventy-five books in eight series including: Zoe Donovan Cozy Mysteries, Whales and Tails Island Mysteries, Sand and Sea Hawaiian Mysteries, Tj Jensen Paradise Lake Series, Writers' Retreat Southern Seashore Mysteries, Rescue Alaska Paranormal Mysteries, and Seacliff High Teen Mysteries. Find out more about her books at www.kathidaley.com

Giveaway:

I do a giveaway for books, swag, and gift cards every week in my newsletter, *The Daley Weekly* **http://eepurl.com/NRPDf**

Other links to check out:

Kathi Daley Blog – publishes each Friday **http://kathidaleyblog.com**

Webpage – **www.kathidaley.com**

Facebook at Kathi Daley Books – **www.facebook.com/kathidaleybooks**

Kathi Daley Books Group Page –
**https://www.facebook.com/groups/5695788231468
50/**

E-mail – **kathidaley@kathidaley.com**

Goodreads –
**https://www.goodreads.com/author/show/7278377.
Kathi_Daley**

Twitter at Kathi Daley@kathidaley –
https://twitter.com/kathidaley

Amazon Author Page –
https://www.amazon.com/author/kathidaley

BookBub –
https://www.bookbub.com/authors/kathi-daley

Pinterest – **http://www.pinterest.com/kathidaley/**

Made in the USA
Middletown, DE
31 October 2018